D1535459

Pure
of Heart

DISNEY MIRRORVERSE

Pure of Heart

NEW YORK TIMES BEST-SELLING AUTHOR

Delilah S. Dawson

DISNEY PRESS

Los Angeles • New York

Printed in the United States of America

First Hardcover Edition, July 2023

10 9 8 7 6 5 4 3 2 1

FAC-004510-23131

Library of Congress Control Number: 2022942667

ISBN 978-1-368-07891-7

Illustrations by Clara Tessier
Design by Scott Piehl
Visit disneybooks.com

SUSTAINABLE FORESTRY INITIATIVE

Certified Sourcing

www.forests.org
SFI-01681

Logo Applies to Text Stock Only

Pure of Heart

Introduction

———◇———

In the not very distant past, two magical stars collided, sending reality spiraling in two very different directions.

The Source Worlds you know and love still exist, but now our beloved characters also exist as new, amplified versions of themselves in the Mirrorverse. In the Mirror Worlds, everything is heightened—personalities, powers, and dangers! These fantastic versions of classic Disney characters will possess new magical powers, new weapons, new gear, and new discoveries about the roles they'll play in a transformed world.

After the stellar collision, the Snow White of our

own fairy tale continued with her time line at the cottage of her seven dear friends in the way that we all know. But in Snow White's Mirror World, things have changed—drastically. The Mirrorverse Snow White begins her own story at that same cottage, but nothing will ever be the same. . . .

1

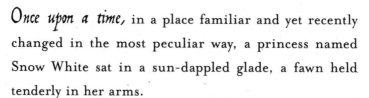

Once upon a time, in a place familiar and yet recently changed in the most peculiar way, a princess named Snow White sat in a sun-dappled glade, a fawn held tenderly in her arms.

"I wish you could tell me how you broke your leg," she said, wrapping the delicate limb in a length of cloth so that the splint she'd made could help the growing bones heal. "The forest is such a dark and dangerous place these days."

The other forest animals crept close as if the princess was the only source of warmth and safety in all the world. Fuzzy rabbits nuzzled up against her leg, birds hopped and twittered on her shoulders, and the fawn's mother fretted as she oversaw the procedure, occasionally nudging the princess in the back with her wet black nose. Once Snow White was satisfied with her work, she helped the fawn to stand and clapped her hands as it wobbled around the clearing, doing its very best to frolic.

"Oh, that's so much better! You really will be fine, you know. You just have to be careful for a few weeks, until it doesn't hurt a bit. Then we'll take off the splint, and—"

She kicked away a vine that seemed almost to be angling for the fawn's spindly legs, trying to trip the tiny creature. The glossy green leaves were threaded with purple . . . well, not veins. Cracks, really. Snow White had noticed the cracks here and there in the woodland recently, and every time she tried to inspect one of the leaves more closely, it slithered away.

"Just be careful, won't you?" The fawn continued to frolic, and Snow White looked to the doe standing guard. "Keep him close. Something is wrong here, but I can't quite put my finger on it."

The doe inclined her head in understanding and stepped closer to her charge.

"Goodbye! Goodbye to all of you! And please, do watch yourselves. The forest is changed, and not for the better."

Picking up her basket of supplies, Snow White glanced up at the afternoon sun slanting through the trees. A chill wind blew, rustling her cloak and reminding her that dark would soon fall. Even before things had grown strange, the forest had never been a safe place to be at night. All the animals knew where to seek shelter, and she didn't want to be out on the twisting paths alone. She had no weapons, wouldn't even know how to use one. Although her forest friends seemed to understand her better than ever, she thought she'd seen people hunting between the trees. Among them was her wicked stepmother's huntsman, no doubt. But was he searching for Snow White at the Queen's behest, or was he on some other sinister business shrouded in secrecy?

Snow White shivered. She didn't want to find out.

As she hurried along the trail, branches whipped into her face, showering her with rattling leaves and plucking at her cloak and hair with wicked thorns tipped in purple. She batted them away and hurried faster, the wind howling like an animal denied its prey. It felt as if she held her breath all the way back to the home of her dear friends. When she finally saw the sloping straw roof and glinting windows of the snug cottage, she sighed in relief, dreaming of the hearty stew she'd left to warm upon the hearth.

But wait.

Something was . . . wrong.

Her friends should've been home from the mine already, and the windows should have glowed cheerfully with their lanterns as their voices floated out the open door to the tune of Grumpy's organ. Instead, the house sat cold and dark, the open door banging angrily in the breeze.

"Hello?" Snow White called at the threshold, placing her basket out of the way. "Happy? Grumpy? Sneezy? Sleepy? Bashful? Doc? Dopey? Are you here?"

At least one of them should've called out to answer her, but the house was unnaturally silent.

Goose bumps rose along her arms, and she fumbled with the fire striker, lighting the lanterns and candles one by one until she could assure herself that the downstairs was exactly as she'd left it.

Well, except for the fire. That had gone out, leaving the stew thick and cold.

"Oh, no," Snow White muttered. "That won't do."

She knelt at the hearth, building a little stack of kindling and straw to carefully tend the tiny new flame she had created.

Something creaked on the stairs, and she spun around, eyes wide.

No one was there.

"Old houses, I suppose," she said to herself, because hearing a voice made the empty cottage seem just a little bit friendlier. "The castle used to make such strange noises, back before the Queen sent me away with her huntsman. The creaks and cracks, the wind in the stone. And always so damp. Why, I don't miss it a bit!"

She glanced over her shoulder again and again as she worked to get the fire going, positively certain that someone was watching even though she couldn't see them. Maybe there was a shy little mouse somewhere, waiting for crumbs.

Once she was satisfied that the stew would soon be warm again and ready to nourish her friends after a long day in the mine, she went upstairs to check that nothing was out of place there, taking a candle with her. After all, with the door wide open, anyone might've come in.

Shadows danced on the walls as she crept up the stairs, listening for any sound of her friends. Much to her surprise, she found them already in their beds and under their covers, although it was barely suppertime.

"Goodness, are you asleep already? And without dinner?" she said to the seven shadowy lumps. "I don't think I've ever seen you miss dinner before."

There was no answer. And in that silence, she realized something so strange and shocking that ice trickled down her spine.

Not one of them was snoring.

Usually, she could hear her friends from downstairs, and typically standing among them in this room was like listening to seven logs being sawn by seven sneezing bears with head colds.

But now, the room was utterly silent, utterly still.

Holding her candle aloft, Snow White tiptoed up to Dopey's bed.

"Now, Dopey, I know you always want to be the first at the table—"

But as she lifted the patched blanket to reveal his nightcapped bald head, she found something unexpected, something that made no sense, something altogether terrifying.

Her friend Dopey didn't look like himself at all. He had turned a sinister shade of purple, and when he opened his eyes, they glowed an empty, evil white.

"Bring me the heart of Snow White," he said.

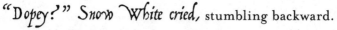

2

"Dopey?" Snow White cried, stumbling backward.

Because the thing about Dopey, of course, was that he didn't speak. He had never spoken a single word. And now . . .

"Bring me the heart of Snow White," he said again, and it wasn't at all the sort of voice she would've expected based on his laughter and sighs.

Dopey—or the creature who looked like Dopey—with purple skin flickering and eyes glowing, rose like a puppet pulled by its strings. The covers slithered off the bed, and he leapt up on top of the mattress, looming over her, hands going to fists.

"Bring me the heart of Snow White!" the creature growled.

"I don't know what's happening, but I don't think it's funny at all," Snow White said, edging toward the door. "If this is some sort of prank, why, why, I don't believe I approve!"

The Dopey look-alike leapt to the ground, hunched over, leering as he staggered toward her. She realized he was holding a weapon—an axe! As she kept backing away, she ran up against Doc's bed, the heavy, hand-hewn wood barking against her spine.

"Bring me the heart of Snow White!"

This time, the voice came from behind her, and she spun around to find Doc standing on the bed, the same shade of purple as Dopey, his once-kind eyes burning white and filled with cruelty behind his glasses. To Snow White's absolute horror, he raised a sword overhead, grinning as the blade arced toward her.

With a speed and agility she hadn't known she possessed, she sidestepped the edge and spun away toward the door. She knew she should run, knew something was desperately wrong, and yet . . . they were her friends. They'd offered safety and understanding in her time of need and had helped her overcome the pain of losing her former life after the Queen had sent her off to die . . . to be killed.

Something had happened to her friends, and she had to help them.

As she faced the two rows of beds, the five others crawled out from under their covers, each the same corrupt shade of purple, crackling with energy as if lightning lived restless under their skin. All their eyes, once brown and kind—well, except for Grumpy, whose eyes were always grumpy—were the same glowing white, empty and evil. Each of her friends held a new weapon she'd never seen them with before, axes and bows and halberds and swords. Dopey stalked toward her without a hint of his usual clumsiness, axe raised in his hands, and Doc jumped to the ground with a cat's grace, the sword held as if he knew how to use it.

"Bring me the heart of Snow White," they all chanted in perfect unison.

"No!" she shouted.

Spinning around, she ran for the stairs, taking them three at a time to escape—well, whatever had happened to her friends. Maybe they'd all eaten the wrong mushroom, or been infected by some kind of strange magic, but they clearly wanted to hurt her, which was very much out of character. When she hit the last stair, she scurried for the front door, but of course she'd closed and locked it when she came in. As she reached for the door handle, an arrow thwacked into the wood, just inches from her hand. She snatched back her hand and looked up to find a purple Bashful acting not bashful at all as he nocked another arrow.

"I don't know what's come over you, but you're all being terribly rude!" she said. "Why, I think—"

She ducked as another arrow barely missed her head and slammed into the door behind her. It was so close she felt the wind whisper in her hair. Snow White had never considered herself to be particularly nimble or quick, and yet it was almost as if she could sense the incoming attacks, for all that they made no sense.

"Bring me the heart of Snow White!" Happy said, and those were the least happy words he'd ever spoken.

Another arrow slammed into the ground, pinning Snow White's skirt, and something turned in her heart like a key clicking in a lock.

These were not her friends.

Her real friends would never cause her harm, not for all the diamonds in the world.

Whoever these terrible purple fellows were, they wanted to hurt her—to genuinely hurt her, possibly even kill her.

And she wasn't going to let that happen.

Ripping her skirt to free herself from the arrow, she lunged for the nearest weapon—an old pickaxe with a loose handle that needed mending. The wood felt good in her hands, solid and sure, and she swung it at the nearest attacker, a sure hit that thudded up her arms. But instead of crying out like one of her friends surely would—like Sleepy would have—the wretched thing just sparked with purple energy and teal lightning, absorbing the hit and taking a step back to raise his axe. Before he could strike, Snow White hit him with the pickaxe again, this time putting more of her strength behind it, determined to make it count.

Crash!

Sleepy—the purple version of Sleepy—the terrible, not real, evil, crackling version of Sleepy who was trying to hurt her—

He shattered like a broken glass, purple shards raining down to clatter on the wooden floorboards of the kitchen.

The horrid thing that had pretended to be Sleepy was gone.

Snow White choked back a sob, the pickaxe falling from her hands.

What had she done?

She'd never hurt a living thing in her entire life, and she'd just fought with a creature that looked like one of her dearest friends, and now he was gone.

"You weren't Sleepy," she told herself. "Sleepy would never—"

"Bring me the heart of Snow White!"

Some new instinct made her instantly drop to the ground, and a sword slashed overhead, right where her middle had been. The imposter version of Happy stood over her, flashing purple, raising his sword for a downward stroke. Why had she let go of the pickaxe? There were seven of them, after all, not just one, and with one gone, that left six who wanted to hurt her.

Snow White rolled to the side and grabbed a hammer that lay beside a sturdy red toolbox. When the sword arced down, she rolled again, and the blade sank into the wood floor. As the purple Happy tried to yank it free, she stood and swung the hammer, flinching from the impact. It was as if this creature too wasn't made of flesh and bone, but was hard and brittle and empty. He didn't respond to the strike, didn't so much as grunt, and she hit him again and again until he, too, exploded in a cascade of crackling violet shards.

This time, instead of dropping her weapon, she kept the hammer in hand—and reached for the pickaxe with her other hand. Five creatures against one inexperienced, frightened young woman meant her odds still weren't good. But whatever these beings were, they weren't very smart—they could say only the one line, and they seemed to take turns attacking instead of piling on all at once.

Good. She could use that to her advantage.

The creature who resembled Bashful came at her next, the confidence in his attack offering further proof that these purple monsters were not her dear friends. As he aimed his arrow at her chest, she dodged and landed hits with her hammer and pickaxe, feeling a new strength flow through her body, the weapons singing in her hands. With a few quick blows, he was nothing but a pile of purple shards crackling with energy.

As she turned to look for her next foe, an arrow landed in her shoulder, the white-hot pain of it shocking. She gasped and dropped her weapons. She'd never been hit before, never suffered a worse injury than a stubbed toe or fire-singed finger, and for a moment, she could only stand there and gawp at the arrow in her arm.

"Bring me the heart of Snow White!" the purple Grumpy said as he started to reload his bow.

She frowned and yanked out the arrow, then plucked up her weapons as she strode toward him. Her shoulder burned hot, but that only made her fight twice as hard, knowing that these creatures weren't playing, that they truly wanted to do her harm. Before he could pull back his bowstring, Snow White took down the fake Grumpy with her pickaxe and hammer. This time, she was ready for the next attack before the purple shards clattered to the ground.

"Bring me the heart of Snow White!" Sneezy said, axe drawn back, but Snow White was already running for him, determined and certain. The weapons felt good in her hands, and it was as if she'd always known how to use them, as if rather than being everyday tools that her friends often left lying around the kitchen, these objects had been handmade specifically for her. After a few deft hits, the fake Sneezy fell.

As Snow White focused in on the not-Doc, something slammed into her back, a searing slash of heat. The weapons flew out of her hands to clatter on the floor as she reached for her back, finding—well, she'd worry about that later. The fight wasn't done.

When she spun around, rigid with pain, the breath knocked out of her, she found the fake Dopey holding an axe.

"Bring me the heart of Snow White," he said, and it was sickening, those words coming out of Dopey's mouth.

"Never!" she shouted.

She dove for her weapons, hammer in her left hand and pickaxe in her right, and twisted onto her back, crossing the weapons in front of her just as Dopey's axe slammed downward. As the blade struck, there was a flash of light, bright and clear as a star, along with a pulse of power that threw the false Dopey backward and into a wall. When the light faded, she saw that something impossible had happened.

Her weapons had . . . changed.

The simple, small pickaxe and hammer had merged into a larger, stronger, stranger pickaxe altogether, a mythic tool that seemed forged by the forest itself. The handle was solid polished wood with the burls and curls of a mighty branch. The blade shimmered indigo, the earth's precious minerals hammered and hardened into a gleaming curve with sharpened points. As she touched the woodgrain, pink and red flowers sprang up in the wake of her fingertip. This new pickaxe was almost as tall as she was! The moment Snow White's fingers closed around the handle, the weapon gleamed and seemed to flow with power.

She spun to where Dopey and Doc approached, leaping into the air and slashing down with the blade. It sang as it arced down, a noise like roots joyously bursting through stone, and both enemies fell back. Hacking, jabbing, parrying, leaping, spinning, she wielded the weapon like it was an extension of her body until, with one bright flash, the last two fake versions of her friends shattered into a thousand shimmering purple shards.

Snow White groaned as she stood tall, weapon still clutched in her hands. She couldn't stop glancing into every corner of the room, her eyes snapping to every shadow, hunting for yet another foe.

But they were all gone, reduced to nothing more than violet fragments. As she watched, those shards disappeared before her very eyes, leaving nothing behind, not a single sign that they'd ever existed at all.

"Happy, Dopey, Doc, Sleepy, Sneezy, Bashful, Grumpy?" Snow White called into the empty cottage. "Are you here? You can come out now. Those horrid things are gone."

But there was no answer. Nothing moved. When she limped upstairs, she couldn't find any evidence at all, other than unmade beds, that the sinister purple monsters had ever existed.

"But what were they?" she said to herself. "And where are my real friends?"

Downstairs, a sound.

The door creaking open.

"Hello?" an unfamiliar voice called.

Clutching her pickaxe, aching and hurt, Snow White tiptoed down the stairs and leapt out into the light, brandishing her weapon.

"Who are you, and where are my friends?" she cried.

Much to her surprise, a strange figure with huge round ears stood there in sparkling robes of gold and white. His conical gold hat was covered in glowing moons, and his cloak glimmered with swirling stars, as if it contained a galaxy.

"I'm Mickey Mouse," he said with a charming grin. "And I don't know where your friends are, but we're going to find out. Together."

3

Snow White was well accustomed to being surrounded by the cheerful and curious creatures of the forest, but in all her days she'd never imagined serving tea to a giant talking animal.

"Do you take sugar?" she asked.

"Yes, please." Mickey held out his cup. "And maybe some cream?"

She poured his cup and then her own and placed the cream and sugar pots near her guest. After the chaos she'd faced in the fight, there was something comforting about the everyday actions of making tea. Her hand shook as she drained her cup and poured a second one, standing all the while.

"Please sit," Mickey said, pushing out a chair with what had to be magic. "I'm sure you've got a lot of questions."

But she couldn't sit. Snow White was full of nervous energy, and she hated to see remnants of what had happened in the disarray of the cottage. "Oh, I'm afraid I can't sit down right now." She finished her second cup and began to pace nervously around the kitchen. "But I need to know: what were those . . . those creatures? I know they weren't my dear friends."

Mickey put down his teacup and leaned forward. "Were they purple and crackling with energy? Did they have blank white eyes that burned? And when you fought them, did they shatter and disappear?"

"Oh, yes!" Snow White stopped to stare at Mickey, her hands clasped tightly together. "Yes, that's it exactly!"

Mickey sat back, nodding knowingly—and a little sadly. "Fractured," he said, and when Snow White gave him a confused look, he added, "I think you need to know the whole story. But rest assured, they were not your friends. You . . . really might want to sit down for this."

Before Snow White took her seat, she poured more tea for them both and fetched some shortbread cookies from under a dish towel. Once she'd had a few bites, she was ready to finally get some answers.

"Things have changed here recently, haven't they?" Mickey began.

"They certainly have!" Snow white nodded eagerly. "At first, it was quite nice. The forest seemed bigger and more beautiful, the colors brighter. Even the water tasted sweeter. But lately . . . well, it's been awful. It's as if the forest has grown darker and more twisted, and dangerous creatures move within it. Paths don't lead where they should. Sometimes it feels like . . . like the forest wants to hurt me! And there are these violet cracks that seem to grow and twist. I thought perhaps I was imagining it, but . . ."

"But it's very real," Mickey agreed with her. "As you've seen today." He ate a piece of shortbread, briefly brightening as he chewed. "Those cracks, that darkness are caused by something called Fractured Magic. It all began with the collision of two stars, one light and one dark."

Mickey stood and waved his hands. A shower of golden sparkles swirled around the kitchen, coalescing into the image of a velvety indigo midnight sky. As he gestured, two stars appeared, one glowing a bold, dazzling white, and the other a malevolent sparking purple. When Mickey brought his hands together, the stars crashed into each other in a huge explosion that made Snow White startle and shield her eyes.

"The two stars collided with such heat and power that two magical mirrors were created. One of those mirrors fell into my world, and a chaotic surge of uncanny power spread throughout the land. That's when I was attacked by magic brooms, if you can believe it." He threw a wary glance at the broom in the corner as if he might never trust such a thing again. "But as I fought them off, I discovered that my own magical powers had been greatly amplified. Since then, I've been studying and learning how to control the energy—the Stellar Magic that exists in my Mirror World. The good magic. That's what originally made your forest brighter. Stellar Magic is what I used to come here—using the Stellar Mirror."

"I don't understand. Those things I fought—that didn't seem like good magic."

Mickey shook his head sadly. "It isn't. The magic from the Stellar Mirror is good, but the dark mirror creates something called Fractured Magic. It infects everything it touches with those purple cracks you've seen. I sensed its influence here and came to help you. I can use Stellar Magic to travel between Mirror Worlds to try to stop the spread of the Fractured Magic and the Fractured."

Snow White's eyes widened. "There are other worlds?"

Mickey sketched an arc with his arms, drawing the shape of a big golden circle. As the magic picture spread, Snow White could see a giant mirror nestled among rocky crags in a world with a swirling, many-colored sky.

"This is the Stellar Mirror in Mirrorforge Crater," Mickey said, awe in his voice. "It was created in the collision, along with various Star Crystals. Using this mirror, I can open portals to other Mirror Worlds. Just as the star collision changed my world, it changed yours, too. You can see the influence of Stellar Magic in the transformation." He looked closer at Snow White. "Have you noticed any changes within yourself lately?"

Snow White considered her hands. "Well, I've always been good with animals, but now it's as if we completely understand each other. It's like they're drawn to me. And when I need something, it's as if the forest hears me and helps me. There was a fawn today with a broken leg, and when I said, 'We're going to need a very straight stick, very sturdy, about this long,' the perfect one just dropped right out of the tree, right at my feet."

"Anything else?"

She looked around the kitchen. "When the . . . Fractured?" Mickey nodded encouragingly. "When they attacked me, I was able to fight back. Why, I've never fought a thing in my entire life, but it was like my body knew what to do, and my mind didn't even think about running away. I surprised myself." She flexed her arm, showing a muscle. "I'm stronger. More agile. More certain." She reached for the sore spot on her shoulder; the arrow's puncture was no longer bleeding. "I seem to heal faster."

Noting her distress, Mickey asked her where she was wounded, and when she showed him her shoulder and back, he used his magic to heal her. The golden sparkles swirled around her, warm as a summer breeze, and then the pain was gone.

"Thank you ever so much!" she exclaimed. "What wonderful magic! I've never been hurt like that before, and I've never so much as picked up an axe, but . . . oh!"

Snow White reached for her newly formed pickaxe and placed it on the table. "I've never used a weapon before today, and then this just . . . happened. I was using a pickaxe and a hammer, and I crossed them to stop the blow of a Fractured axe, and they grew together, like a tree blooming, to save me."

Mickey inspected the pickaxe, eyes shining. "I've seen this happen before. It's part of your powers, your own individual traits amplified by the Stellar Magic. This is a weapon uniquely created by your own personal magic, meant to help fight the Fractured."

Hearing that word again, Snow White's body tensed. "Are there more of them? Do we need to get ready to fight?"

Mickey shook his head. "Not right now. But your instincts are right—where there have been Fractured, you're likely to see even more Fractured. They're created by the Fractured Mirror."

He waved his hands, and the beautiful Stellar Mirror disappeared, replaced by its dark twin. "When the collision happened, it wasn't only the Stellar Mirror that appeared. There was also a Dark Mirror, born from the dark star. But I didn't find that one—an evil wizard named Jafar did. While trying to harness its powers, he broke it, creating the Fractured Mirror. And then a sorceress named Maleficent took control of it and learned to create the Fractured."

Mickey gestured, and a thin, shadowy figure approached the Dark Mirror, which shattered with cracks of the same sinister purple Snow White now knew so well. As she watched in horror, violent creatures popped out of the mirror one after the other: hulking, armored animals holding weapons, their eyes glowing white.

"Whoever possesses the Fractured Mirror can use it, plus the Star Crystals created by the collision, to make Fractured copies of anyone they meet, or endless copies of low-level Fractured goons. Luckily, these mindless, violent monsters can only fight and perform the simplest of actions," Mickey went on. "So that's what you battled here: Fractured copies of your friends."

Snow White stood and took up her pickaxe. "But, then, where are my friends? Did those Fractured—did they . . . hurt . . . ?"

She choked up, unable to finish the question.

"That's what we have to find out together," Mickey said gravely. "If you fought Fractured copies of your friends, that means that whoever has the Fractured Mirror is in this world, and I'm sorry to say this, but they've probably captured your friends. Unless there's anywhere else your friends might be?"

Snow White went to the window and brushed the

curtain aside. Night had fallen, and the darkness out-side was impenetrable. "Oh, no. Not at night. They know very well how dangerous the forest is after dark. They always leave the mine promptly when the cuckoo clock chimes and come straight home." She sighed. "And they never, ever miss a meal, especially when we're having stew."

"Did the Fractured say anything?"

Looking down, Snow White stumbled over the awful words. "They said, 'Bring me the heart of Snow White.'"

Mickey slashed a hand through the air, and the pictures he'd drawn dissolved into sparkles. He leaned forward, looking extremely serious for a creature wearing gold-and-white wizard robes. "Then my next question is this: do you know who in this world would send the Fractured after you, who would send them to take your heart?"

Snow White looked up, angry and hurt, as always when speaking on this subject. "It can only be my step-mother, the Queen. She once sent me out into the forest with her huntsman, and I suppose she gave him orders to—to—" She shook her head. "He raised his knife up, and I was trapped, and all I could do was scream. But he was kind, and he couldn't do it, so he let me go."

She glanced at her reflection in the shining blade of her new weapon. "The Queen wants to be the fairest of them all and is consumed with jealousy. As if it matters what I look like! She's always been beautiful, but it was never enough for her." She sighed and put her head in her hands. "I'd hoped she'd forgotten about me once I disappeared, but apparently she still wants me dead."

A fat tear slipped down her cheek, and then another.

Mickey said, "It's not your fault, Snow White. Some people are driven by terrible emotions, and it would appear the Fractured Magic only amplified her dangerous traits. As much as I hate to say it, she'll probably send more Fractured after you until she gets her way."

Sweeping away her tears, Snow White put her pickaxe down and then placed her hands on the table. "Then what do we do? How do we fight her? Because I don't mind if she comes after me—she's been trying to hurt me for years—but I will not allow her to harm my friends."

Mickey stood, flicking the shortbread crumbs off his robes and tossing back the dregs of his tea. "The only way to stop Fractured Magic is to fight it," he said. "And as this is your world, you have unique abilities and powers that will help you find and stop the Fractured Mirror."

Full of energy but a little unsure, Snow White looked down at her hands. They were petite hands that could bake pies or carry water from the well, but not hands that had ever grown calluses from wielding an axe or a hammer. "But what can I do?" she said, her voice small. "I'm just one person."

Mickey took her hands and looked into her eyes. "Know this: just one person is all it takes to stand up to evil." He smiled a lopsided smile. "But you don't have to go it alone. Come with me, and I'll introduce you to the Guardians."

"The Guardians?" Snow White said. "Who are they?"

Mickey stuffed the last shortbread cookies in his pocket and handed Snow White her weapon. "Join me in Mirrorforge Crater and I'll show you."

◇

4

Mickey led Snow White outside, guiding their way with a dancing flame held in his palm. Although the forest still seemed to curl in wickedly as if waiting to snap up Snow White in one mighty gulp, Mickey moved confidently, the fire lighting a path through the shadows. The purple-tinged leaves seemed to shrink away from him, as if sensing the Stellar Magic's goodness. Soon they stood in a small clearing, facing a miniature version of the Stellar Mirror from Mickey's magical vision. The gold-rimmed portal floated gently in midair, reflecting a different world within.

"Do I just step in?" Snow White asked, both frightened and excited.

"Ha ha! Yep, just hop in. It might feel a little funny at first, but it doesn't hurt."

She walked forward and began to feel a sort of pull, almost like a sunny wind tugging playfully. "Maybe you should go first?"

Mickey offered her a gentle smile. "You're braver than you know, Snow White. This is your first step into a whole new world."

Snow White had never considered her own bravery; up until her skirmish with the Fractured, she'd never imagined herself a fighter. But she couldn't just stand there—not while her friends were in trouble. She had to take the first step, as Mickey had said.

Tentatively, holding her pickaxe in one hand, she stepped closer to the mirror and reached out to put a hand on the shifting gold frame. "Do I—"

But she didn't get a chance to finish her sentence. It felt as if someone had tied a rope of sunshine around her waist, and it tugged her forward with a peculiar enthusiasm. The forest disappeared, and colors swirled around her—formless but beautiful, like sunlight on water, but in shades of magenta, cyan, and cerulean. She wasn't sure whether it was safe to breathe, so she held her breath and clutched her weapon. The magical pictures Mickey had shown her suggested that Mirrorforge Crater was a safe, pretty place, but . . . well, lately, all the places she'd considered safe had taken a turn for the sinister.

Right as she ran out of breath, she was thrown into the air with the energy of a bubble popping. But her body didn't flail; it was as if she already knew exactly what to do. Angled forward, perfectly balanced, she landed on the ground, kneeling, her weapon held at the ready.

She stood slowly, taking in the glory of this new world, and realized she was seeing a place that might as well be on the moon, it was so very different from everything she'd ever known. There were no forests here, no animals, no adorable little thatched cottages—just swirling colors and jagged stones, with the sky glowing an imperial indigo overhead. Behind her, the Stellar Mirror pulsed like an opal made of fire and water both, an exquisite living jewel that filled her with awe.

Truly, this thing, this place—they were made of stars! The universe was so much greater than she'd ever dreamed, and to think that she was a part of it. She was stunned and humbled . . . and excited to play her role.

"Well, hello," someone said, and Snow White jerked

her head around to find a young woman about her age sitting on a rock, watching her with amused curiosity. She had warm brown skin and wore a moss-green coat over leggings along with lace-up brown boots. Straps and bags crisscrossed her chest, waist, and knees, with bottles and tubes full of vibrantly colored liquids stuffed into every available location. There was a beautiful butter-yellow water lily holding back her coiled, shoulder-length hair and another flower pinned to her coat.

Snow White straightened up, feeling a little unsure—and out of place. Before she could respond to the greeting, Mickey appeared, landing lightly on the stone in a swirl of his golden robes.

"Ah! Tiana! Just the person I was hoping to see!" he called in greeting.

The young woman instantly turned serious. "We got a problem?"

Mickey beckoned Snow White over. "Snow White, this is Tiana, one of our finest Guardians. Tiana, this is Snow White. We've just confirmed that the Fractured Mirror is in her world, and it's already taking its toll."

Tiana's expression softened sympathetically at the mention of the Fractured Mirror. "I'm so sorry, sugar.

That mirror sure can make a pretty place mean." She looked to Mickey. "Do we know who has it?"

But instead of answering, Mickey looked to Snow White.

With all their attention focused on her, Snow White had to be brave. "My stepmother, the Queen. Well, in my head, I'm afraid I think of her as the *wicked* queen. That's what my friends call her, too. She's certainly done enough to earn the name."

"Snow White was attacked by Fractured that looked like her friends," Mickey explained. "And she managed to fight off seven of them at once, even though she'd never held a weapon before or had any training. Can you believe it?"

Tiana smirked, but sweetly. "I sure can. Looks like you have a mighty fine weapon, too." She gestured at Snow White's pickaxe, still held at the ready.

Feeling a little silly, Snow White slung the blade over her shoulder. "Oh, yes, it was so peculiar. I was fighting with a hammer and a pickaxe, and then there was an axe, and—well, this is what they all became."

"Are you going to be a—" Tiana began, but she was interrupted by something heavy landing on the ground behind them.

Snow White spun around to find a terrifying monster towering over her, a mass of blue-and-purple fur covered in hard yellow armor. The beast had curling horns and huge claws, and it opened its foul mouth, showing gleaming white teeth—

And sneezed.

"'Scuse me," the monster said, rubbing his blue nose.

Tiana laughed—at the monster!—and said, "Sulley, I still can't believe you're allergic to Mirrorforge Crater."

"I used to think a baby sock could kill me," the monster—Sulley—admitted. "So I guess I'll take a slight allergy to multidimensional star portals any day."

"Snow White, this is James P. Sullivan," Mickey said.

"But my friends call me Sulley." The monster smiled and held out a paw, and even though she was still slightly terrified, Snow White shook it, noting that his fur was much softer than she had ever imagined a monster could be.

"Pleased to meet you," she said. "Are you a . . . a sort of turtle?"

Sulley looked slightly surprised and stared down at himself. "Oh, this? Yeah, it's not a shell. It's armor. I had my team back home at Monsters, Inc., look into some cutting-edge door technology to build this defensive shield. If you're ever in trouble, just hide behind me. I'm pretty much a big fuzzy wall."

"Unless you make him mad, and then you have to face the side with all the teeth and claws," Tiana said teasingly.

"Oh, I would never!" Snow White exclaimed.

Sulley looked sheepish. "As long as you're not a Fractured goon or one of the bad guys who spawn them, you're pretty safe."

"He's just a big ol' kitten," Tiana added with a hip bump that didn't nudge Sulley an inch.

"Oh! Who has a kitten?"

A new person had appeared, another young woman—but a very different one, with golden hair so long Snow White couldn't find the end of it. She wore a short dress of mauve and plum over matching leggings, with gleaming copper armor over her chest and left arm. Her blond hair swirled around with every movement as if it had a mind of its own, and her feet were bare. Much to Snow White's surprise, the woman held, of all things, a frying pan.

"Just talking about Sulley," Tiana said. "How you doin', Punz?"

"Ha ha, very funny," the newcomer said, rolling her

eyes with a smile. "You know, when you call me that, it makes me think you are under the impression I just make bad puns all the time. But I only make bad puns some of the time."

"And you're not *kitten*," Tiana replied.

"Oh!" the young woman laughed, her face brightening further; it seemed like she was probably bright and sunny all the time. "Good one!" She stepped up to Snow White, moving her massive coil of golden hair out of the way. "I'm Rapunzel. And this is Pascal. He usually stays back home in my world, but he was up for an adventure today." A tiny green chameleon poked up from under the armor on her shoulder, gave a salute, and disappeared. "And this is my frying pan. It doesn't have a name. Wait. Should it have a name?"

"I'm Snow White, and . . . I tend to name things only when the moment strikes."

Rapunzel grinned. "Yes! I like that. Make the frying pan earn its name in battle."

Snow White looked from Rapunzel to Mickey to Tiana to Sulley and couldn't imagine four more unalike people. "So are all the Mirror Worlds the Stellar Mirror leads to so . . . so different?" she asked.

Mickey waved a hand at the mirror, and a ball of

blue fur shot out of the Stellar Mirror as though fired by a cannon and uncurled to reveal a waist-high . . . animal? It wore a tight suit of red and gold and had four arms, antennae, and quills like a porcupine. Its big, inquisitive eyes darted here and there before the creature fell onto all fours—all sixes?—and scrambled toward Mickey. It rose on its back legs to face him and cocked its head.

"Fractured Mirror?" it said in a halting voice.

"That's right, Stitch." Mickey gestured to Snow White and, again, told her story. "Are you willing to join the other Guardians to help her world?"

Stitch scanned her up and down, then sniffed her like a dog hunting for a good scent. She held very still, uncertain of how to interact with this new creature—who had big teeth but whom Mickey had, again, called a Guardian.

"Uh-huh," Stitch said, nodding. "Stitch help fight."

"Stitch is an experimental creature who has risen to prominence in the Galactic Federation," Mickey explained as Stitch sniffed at Snow White's pickaxe. "He doesn't talk much, but he understands everything. In fact, believe it or not, he's a genius, with fighting skills like no other."

Stitch sat down and chewed on one of his back feet for a moment before standing up, looking Snow White in the eye, holding out a hand—paw?—to shake, and saying, "Hi."

"Oh, hello," she answered as he pumped her hand up and down far too many times. "It's very nice to meet you."

"Nice to meet you. Smell like, uh, stew," he said before looking hopefully all around her.

"I left it in my world, I'm afraid," she admitted. "But I do believe we're going back there, and then you're welcome to help yourself." Her smile faltered. "I made it for my friends, you see, and they're . . . they're gone." She began to tear up, and Tiana put a comforting arm around her shoulders.

"Don't worry," Tiana said with a squeeze. "With a team like this, there's no way we can lose."

"Oh, I don't know," someone new said, voice dripping with sarcasm. "I can think of plenty of ways you could lose."

Everyone turned in surprise to find a tall sort of man with craggy blue skin and fire for hair. A smoky shadow swirled around him like a gray tunic, his armored shoulders curled up like horns, and when he smiled, it was cruel. Since everyone else's arrival had been met with hugs and handshakes, Snow White was surprised when the others brandished their weapons against him, their faces set in fierce determination.

"Hades," Tiana said coldly. "What are you doing here?"

5

———◇———

"What?" Hades said with a shrug. "It's always 'Guardians this,' 'Guardians that.' You talk it up so much I wanted to find out what it was all about."

"Isn't he a villain?" Tiana asked Mickey, a potion bottle clutched in each hand.

"Villain, schmillain." Hades tried to give a winning smile but didn't quite pull it off. "Just because I'm the god of the land of the dead doesn't mean I want to actually hurt anybody. That's so messy. So much paperwork. I bet no one can even name one horrible thing I've done this century."

"You're the *god* of the *dead*—" Rapunzel began.

"I didn't ask to be!" he shot back. "One brother gets the sky. Oh, good! The sky! Where the stars and birdies are! The other brother gets the ocean, which is full of adorable otters and dolphins and fish. Yay, the ocean! And I get . . . just a bunch of bones and fire, really. Not a great place to host a party."

Mickey stepped between the Guardians and the interloper they all looked ready to battle. "Now, now. Hades wants to see what being a Guardian is all about, and this seemed like a great mission for him to tag along. We've got so much talent on this team, and he has skills that will help you defeat the Fractured influence in Snow White's world. So will you give him a chance?"

"I don't trust him," Tiana said firmly, arms crossed.

Hades spread his hands. "You don't know me yet. Give me some time."

"What if he, I don't know, goes bad?" Rapunzel asked, throwing him major side-eye. "Or sets something on fire? Because I'm pretty sure his hair is fire, and where I come from, fire is dangerous."

"So are frying pans," Hades countered.

"Fair point," Rapunzel agreed.

"If he looks like he might be causing mischief,

then you can detain him," Mickey answered. "Stitch's molecular structure means he can act as a holding cell, basically. Just let me know if there's a problem, and I'll be right there."

"I've always heard you should keep your friends close and your enemies closer," Sulley said.

"Enemies?" Hades's jaw dropped. "But we could be bros! Look at us! Me with my fire, you with your . . . door. We could fight back to back, take on the world!"

Stitch scurried up to Hades and sniffed him before making a face. "Ugh! Rotten eggs!" he said, trying to wipe off his nose with his paws.

"That's sulfur and brimstone, baby," Hades said. "Eau de Underworld. Chicks dig it."

"Snow White, what do you think?" Mickey asked.

Everyone looked to her, and she tried to choose her words carefully; she was new here, and she didn't know exactly how any of this worked. "Well, sometimes first impressions are deceiving, and someone who seems quite wicked really does have a pure heart underneath all their"—she glanced at Hades and quickly looked away again—"bluster. I'm worried for my world and my friends, and I'll take any help we can get. If Mickey trusts him, I'm willing to trust him."

"Belle told me about how—" Tiana started.

"Let's let sleeping dogs lie," Hades interrupted, arms out like he wanted to hug them but didn't quite know how hugs worked. "Especially Cerberus, because he was cranky this morning, and most of you look fairly edible. Three heads need three times the meat, after all." He put his arms down, and everyone, including him, relaxed a little. "So what's the assignment?"

"Tiana, would you mind filling him in?" Mickey asked. She nodded, and Mickey pulled Snow White aside. "Look, I know we want to trust Hades, but Tiana's instincts aren't wrong. He has been considered a bad guy in the past. Look for the best in him and give him a chance to prove himself, but don't forget that he has the potential to be dangerous. Just keep an eye on him and trust your gut, okay?"

"Okay," Snow White agreed. "I can do that."

"Everyone else on the team is proven and solid." Mickey looked on the group with pride. "Talented fighters, skilled healers, born leaders, lab-created superweapons. And I've called upon each one to help protect the Mirrorverse against the threat of the Fractured using their extraordinary abilities. You can count on all of them. The Guardians are committed to protecting the Stellar Magic and driving the Fractured influence out of every world it infects. With this team, you have everything you need."

Snow White looked down. She wasn't sure how to ask this next part, but Mickey seemed like he knew a thing or two about magic, and, well, who else could she ask?

"Mickey, there is one thing I need, if you're able to help . . ." she began.

He smiled and nodded. "I'll do what I can. That's my role here—to support the Guardians and keep watch over Mirrorforge Crater."

She drew a deep breath; asking for things did not come naturally to her, considering she'd been raised practically as a servant under the cruel and watchful eye of her stepmother, the Queen. She held out her torn, ragged skirt.

"It's just . . . everyone else looks so impressive, with their armor and clothes that are made for fighting in. But my dress was ripped in the fight, and my slippers are already wearing through their soles on these rocks. It's just not practical, and everyone else is so formidable, and I feel so ill-equipped beside them. Can your magic . . . well, would it be possible for me to maybe have something better suited to the journey?"

Mickey brightened. "Oh, is that all? Well, of course! Hold still a moment, and I'll see what I can do."

Snow White stood in place, fidgeting self-consciously with her pickaxe as Mickey stepped back and swirled his hands, golden light glittering off his fingertips. The glistening sparkles swirled around her like pollen and petals dancing in a breeze, and it was like she could feel the sunbeams slanting down between the boughs of the trees in her forest back home, before the Fractured magic had infected everything.

As she looked down, the magic started at her toes, replacing her old slippers with sturdy but slender armored boots that would protect her feet, whatever they faced. Her ragged skirts swirled away into nothing, leaving behind comfortable breeches the color of a dirt path through the woods, with a skirt made of autumn leaves in all the prettiest shades of rust and gold. Her new top was blue with a red gem, just like her old one, but it moved easily with her and was thick enough to provide some padding should she take another hit—which she was almost sure now that she would. She especially loved the brass-and-rosewood pauldrons that protected her shoulders and trailed feathers along her upper arms. She touched her hair and found it neatly pulled back by a headband bedecked with two roses.

The golden wind whipped away, and she twirled in place.

"Oh, thank you! It's like it was made just for me!" she said, beaming. "Almost like a gift from the forest—from the way it used to be."

Mickey chuckled. "That's how the Stellar Magic works—it amplifies your own traits, highlighting what's best in you. Your forest is part of you, and so your outfit is drawn from your forest."

"Oh, girl, that is gorgeous!" Tiana said, inspecting Snow White's leafy skirt.

"No place to hang a frying pan, but it really matches your gigantic murder axe," Rapunzel offered with her usual enthusiasm.

"Pretty," Stitch said, nodding.

Even Hades nodded with approval. "Not bad, for something without a single bone embellishment. Skulls are always in season, you know."

Sulley was the only one who hadn't said anything, and he obviously felt pretty awkward about it, so he managed, "Um, yeah, what they said. Minus the skull thing."

"I know I'm not a Guardian," Snow White said,

wondering if she would ever feel as confident in her abilities as these powerful people, "but I'm honored to be part of your team."

"I can't wait to see what you do with that pickaxe." Tiana grinned and tossed a potion bottle in the air, catching it neatly. "Now, who wants to go find that Fractured Mirror?"

A cheer went up, and the Guardians turned toward the Stellar Mirror.

"Everyone ready?" Mickey asked. Tiana nodded, and a look of intense concentration crossed Mickey's face. He stood before the mirror, making big gestures with his hands that made the swirling colors within intensify. As the magic sparked from his fingertips, the colors in the mirror swirled like a vortex, and on the other side, Snow White could see a glimmer of a familiar forest barely lit by starlight.

"What do we need to know?" Sulley asked. "What's in the immediate area?"

"Yeah." Hades squinted into the mirror. "Any monsters, gods, godlings, Titans, fire extinguishers, et cetera?"

"Well . . ." Snow White stared, too. It was so dark on the other side that she could barely see anything. "It's a forest near the home of my friends. We think they were taken by the evil queen, and I had to fight their Fractured versions. There aren't any monsters that I know of—just the general forest creatures. Deer, rabbits, squirrels, birds, turtles. The Queen does send out her hunters, though—lately even more than usual."

"What do they hunt?" Tiana asked.

Snow White sighed deeply. "I think it might be me."

Stitch bristled, the spines on his back quivering. "Eat him!" he barked.

"Oh, I imagine he wouldn't taste good," Snow White said. "He wears lots of leather."

"Forest animals and hunters we can handle." Tiana stepped up. "Sulley, you go first; cover us in case there are Fractured lurking around. Once you've determined it's safe, I want Rapunzel to go, then Stitch, then Snow White, then Hades. I'll join last. Set up a perimeter, and we'll regroup when we're all together. Everybody got it?"

"Got it!" they replied. Snow White didn't reply; she wasn't sure if her voice was loud enough to be included in the count. But she did nod, and that was apparently sufficient.

"Good luck!" Mickey called. "Contact me if there's a problem!"

With a salute, Sulley jumped into the mirror, and Snow White was certain there was no way he could possibly fit, that he would get stuck in there like a cork, but the mirror just sucked him in like a whirlpool, and then he was gone. After a few beats, Tiana gestured for Rapunzel, who dove in headfirst with her hair trailing behind her. Then Stitch leapt through, howling, "Yeah!"

Tiana turned to Snow White. "You ready?"

"Honestly, no," Snow White replied. She looked down at her splendid new costume, at her small white hand clutching the huge weapon. "I'm worried I won't be able to keep up."

"Sure you will!" Mickey said. "You fought seven Fractured all by yourself, caught by surprise. You didn't even know what they were, and you barely took damage. Gosh, Snow White—you're a natural!"

"Mickey's right," Tiana agreed. "Seven Fractured is nothing to sneer at. You're going to do great. And you're not alone—we're in this together. So go on. They're waiting for you." She patted Snow White's back, urging her toward the Stellar Mirror.

This close, Snow White could feel the mirror's pull calling to her. She was scared, but . . . well, she was also excited. She was learning new things about herself, discovering new skills and abilities. And like Tiana said, she wasn't alone. She was part of this group. All these different people, coming together from so many different worlds, all determined to help her world. To help *her*. She couldn't let them down.

"I can do this," she murmured to herself. And then, before she could second-guess it, she walked up to the mirror and jumped.

The colors whirled around her like a soap bubble, and then she landed nimbly in the grass of her own forest clearing, her pickaxe held at the ready.

"No Fractured so far," Sulley murmured as he kept watch. "But this place is definitely under the influence of the Fractured Mirror."

"What do you mean?" Snow White asked.

"All the purple cracks." Rapunzel swatted at a purple-threaded leaf with her frying pan, and the entire branch drew back like it had been burned. "Yuck."

With a slight popping noise, Hades arrived, dusting off his smoke-like robes. "Bit of a fixer-upper, don't you think?" he said, looking around with a sneer. "No fire, no rivers of lava, no screaming souls, no statues of me."

With one last pop, Tiana somersaulted out of the mirror and landed in a crouch.

"What have we got?" she asked as she stood.

"No goons, plenty of purple cracks," Sulley reported.

"Stitch eat squirrels?" Stitch called as his head poked out of the tree overhead.

"Absolutely not!" Snow White stomped a foot. "The forest creatures are not food!"

"Agreed!" Rapunzel said.

"Not even little ones?" Stitch held out a hand, his thumb and first finger almost touching.

"No eating adorable forest animals. Period," Tiana admonished.

Stitch dropped out of the tree with a thump, his ears drooping.

"But there should still be stew," Snow White reminded him, which perked him right back up.

"Which way to the house where you saw the Fractured?" Tiana asked.

Snow White turned slowly in place, trying to get her bearings. "Why, I know this forest by heart, and yet it's changed even more. Recently the trails got twistier, the shadows got darker, but . . . I don't even see one path right now, much less the right one."

Something rustled in the bushes, and Stitch

gleefully shouted, "Squirrel!" before licking his mouth with an extra-huge, extra-slobbery tongue.

"We talked about not eating—" Snow White began.

"Wait."

Snow White looked to where Tiana focused on the rustling bush. It was shaking, and an odd chittering noise made a shiver run up her spine.

"That's not how they usually sound," she admitted. "It's louder. . . ."

Green-tipped claws parted the leaves, and the elongated face that looked out was the size of a wolf's. It hissed, revealing sharp buckteeth.

"Squirrel?" Stitch asked nervously, no longer so hungry.

"That's not . . . how they usually look, either," Snow White said.

The squirrel-thing crawled out of the bush, its bristly, scorpion-like tail tipped with a stinger dripping poisonous green liquid that sizzled where it landed on the ground.

"No purple cracks, no glowing white eyes. It's not Fractured . . ." Rapunzel plucked her frying pan from her hip and took up a defensive position. "But it's not right, either."

"Oh, I can take care of that little guy," Sulley said, holding out his shield, which whined like a machine powering up.

But when five more giant squirrel-scorpions dropped out of the trees, teeth gnashing, Tiana called, "Run!"

And they ran.

6

Snow White didn't think she would be scared returning to her own world, which she knew and understood.
But the changes wrought by the Fractured Mirror had
apparently ramped up, because these were not the
happy little squirrels that had scampered around her
just hours before when she'd fixed the fawn's leg. As she
ran away from the chittering, howling, wolf-sized monsters, she kept her eyes pinned to Tiana's back, knowing
that as long as she wasn't alone, she would be safe.

Well, maybe not safe, but at least she would have a
chance.

The forest herded them down increasingly dark trails, branches grasping for them with sharply tipped twigs, and roots rising to trip them. Snow White wasn't the fastest of the group, and she was grateful that Sulley seemed to be staying right behind her, protecting her from the creatures squeaking and growling furiously at their heels.

CRASH!

A branch fell between Snow White and Tiana, completely blocking the narrow path. Snow White drew up short, hunting for some way to climb over it, but it might as well have been a wall; the smaller branches intertwined like snakes to form a solid mass of thorny greenery. The squirrels skittered up the trees and leapt over them, chasing the larger group instead. Snow White had a brief and troubling thought: more people meant more meat.

"I thought you said your world was more normal," Sulley called, trying in vain to rip the branches apart with his hands.

"It used to be," Snow White called back. "But even this is different. There were purple cracks before, but the poisonous sort of green is new."

"I guess it's nice to stay busy."

Sulley definitely sounded doubtful.

After a few moments, he gave up attacking the tree and turned to Snow White, worry written across his features. Funny how the first time she'd seen him she'd thought him a ferocious monster, when clearly he was a big softy, at least toward his friends.

"We'll have to backtrack and find another path," he said. "This tree just will not budge!"

Snow White turned, surveying the area all around.

"There! A break in the foliage. Maybe it will lead us around."

"It's in the wrong direction, but hopefully we'll find the real path once we're out in the open." Sulley's huge shoulders hunched. "Seems like our best option. Want me to go first?"

Snow White shook her head and hefted her pickaxe. "It's a tight fit. I'll go first, you protect my back in case the squirrels return. If you don't mind?"

Sulley bowed. "After you."

Ducking under the branches, Snow White stepped onto the new trail, and the temperature went shockingly cold under the shadows. There wasn't a lot of room to maneuver, and the path was so twisty that she couldn't see what was up ahead. As she moved, she heard the leaves press back to make enough room for Sulley. It was almost as if the forest *wanted* them to go this way. But why?

"You know, we don't really have forests like this back home," Sulley said nervously. "I live in a big city. Most of our trees are planted in the sidewalk and trimmed regularly." The leaves rustled away from him in alarm. "Yeah, I know. It does sound a little confining. I was kind of excited to see a world that was mostly forest, but now . . ."

Snow White stepped over a big root, glad she had more secure footwear thanks to Mickey's magic. Maybe Rapunzel could fight barefoot, but she certainly didn't want to. "It used to be very nice, this forest. I was frightened of it at first, because it looked scary, but once I saw it for what it really was, it became a lovely haven."

"Always nice to meet someone who's not judgmental—" Sulley began, but then he went utterly silent. When Snow White looked behind her, the big blue monster had disappeared.

From Sulley's point of view, there had been ground, and then there wasn't. He was so surprised that he didn't scream, didn't roar. He just quietly said, "Oh!" and plummeted.

It was dark, this strange pit he was falling through, darker than midnight, and before he even had time to flail, he landed with a mighty splash in sludge up to his waist.

"What is this place?" he said to himself as he stood, because he'd been staring directly at Snow White when the ground gave out, and she'd been standing on a seemingly solid path. Still, it felt friendly to say the words out loud, even if there was no one there to reply. If his friend Mike Wazowski had been there, silence would not have been an option, but Sulley was utterly alone—not his favorite way to be.

"Hello?" he called, because maybe someone else from the team had likewise fallen down a—a what? A pit? Quicksand? If so, it was exceptionally quick, because he hadn't even noticed the ground disappearing until it was gone.

No one answered at first . . . but then, someone did.

"You let her down," a voice said.

Sulley spun around in the thick, black water to find the voice's owner, and something slammed into his jaw, knocking him backward. When he struggled up to standing, dripping viscous sludge, he found an armored alligator holding a wizard's staff topped with a ball of light that lit the fetid swamp in tones of wicked violet.

A Fractured goon.

No problem for James P. Sullivan, top scarer of Monstropolis and specially chosen Guardian of—

Whack!

Something smashed into Sulley's back, and he spun again, finding an identical alligator goon holding another wizard's staff.

"She was counting on you," this one hissed.

But Sulley knew about Fractured goons, knew they could say one thing and one thing only, and that it was usually something nasty.

"And she can keep counting on me!" he shouted, winding back to wallop the second gator with his techno-boosted force smash.

The gator flew back, the watery sludge spouting up like ink when it landed.

"You let her down," the first gator said, almost cloying, and Sulley roared and punched it with all his power, throwing it across the darkness.

Sulley followed it, and with another two hits, that gator went down in a shower of crystals that sank under the surface. But then the pack on Sulley's back began to spark and hiss. The water must've gotten into the containment system. If he didn't get out of there, all his tech would fry, and he would be even more useless than he was now.

"You lost her," said a third gator, and it was right, he had lost her—poor Snow White was alone in the darkest shadows of a sinister forest, trapped, hopefully not crying, probably hurt, not knowing anything about the Fractured, not knowing anything about her powers or how to fight, only knowing that someone wanted to hurt her, and with Sulley gone, they would probably succeed—

"She was counting on you!"

Sulley's eyes flicked back and forth from one gator to the other, two identical, brainless enemies saying the same horrible thing over and over again.

You lost her.

She was counting on you.

You lost her.

It was too much. Sulley had smashed plenty of goons, but always with a team, always with help. He held up his shield, but it didn't gear up and hum with power, didn't respond as it should've, the perfect weapon for striking back at these Fractured freaks. He lashed out with just an arm, but the goon barely budged.

"She was counting on you," it said again.

And Sulley thought back to discovering that his old boss, Mr. Waternoose, was actually the bad guy, and how at first it had seemed completely insurmountable, fighting against the most powerful monster in Monstropolis. He'd felt so hopeless, so helpless, like as big as he was, even he wasn't big enough to win against such horrible odds. But then his friends had stepped in, and together, they'd built new tech that Waternoose had never even dreamed of.

He had friends, at home and among the Guardians.

He could return to them.

He just had to get on the other side of these goons and find them.

He hadn't let Snow White down.

Not yet.

"You lost her," the alligator said in that dead voice, rearing back to strike.

"Then I'll find her again!" Sulley roared, teeth bared, and even without the extra crackle of his shield's full capabilities, his strike was so powerful that the gator soared through the air and splashed back down feet away.

"She was—" the other gator started, but Sulley silenced it with a mighty punch.

"She *is* counting on me! And I'm fine with that!"

A few more punches and that gator exploded in a cloud of purple crystals that sank into the water and disappeared. If the third gator had had a mind, if it had been anything but a useless copy of a copy of a goon, it would've run for its life. But as things stood, it was just bad intentions trapped in crystal by dark magic, and Sulley destroyed it with his huge fists.

"Don't tell me how it is!" he shouted between strikes. "I'm going to find her!"

Smash!

The last gator disappeared, and Sulley exhaled in relief and then cracked his back. His feet were cold; the water was seeping into every bit of his fur. It was probably all matted down like a wet cat.

"Embarrassing," he grumbled, trying to smooth his fur out of his eyes.

With the Fractured goons and their sickly violet light gone, he was starting to be able to see down here, but there wasn't much to be seen. Just dark water and twisted roots hanging down.

He could work with that.

Wishing for Stitch's ability to change his molecular structure, Sulley reached for some nearby roots dangling from far overhead and tested their strength. They seemed solid enough, although the purple cracks made him nervous.

"Should've done this more in gym class," he murmured as he pulled himself up, hand over hand, his tail dangling as his feet curled around the wormy root.

Up and up he went, feeling every pound of his mass, regretting his big breakfast. Every moment, he expected to hear the hideous hiss of another freakish foe or feel the violet-threaded vine twist in his hands, its Fractured magic seeking to hurt anything that pulsed with Stellar influence. But the roots stayed roots, the vines stayed vines, and soon he saw scant light overhead, just enough to give him hope that he was almost out.

"Sulley!" Snow White shouted happily. "Are you all right? I was so worried!"

"I'm okay," he said tiredly, dragging himself up out of the hole and onto the ground. "But I wouldn't recommend going down there. Not the friendliest folks, those Fractured goons."

"There were Fractured down there?" she asked, shocked.

Sulley shrugged. "Wherever the Fractured Mirror

is, somebody's going to be using it to try to take over. That's just how it works. They make goons, the goons attack, we fight back." He straightened up and cracked his neck. "And then we get healed, so let's find the rest of the team. That was a long fall, and I'm pretty sure I look like a wet rug."

Snow White sniffed, tried not to make a face . . . and failed. "I'm sure it will wash out. Once we get to the cottage, I have some lovely rose soap."

"Rose soap." He shook his head. "I don't understand the human sense of smell. Do you know what people would pay for this Eau d'Swamp in Monstropolis? I could bottle that water and sell it."

Snow White chuckled. "Monstropolis sounds like a very different place indeed. I hope I'll get to see it one day."

Sulley shrugged. "If you become a Guardian and someone takes the Fractured Mirror there, you might get a chance. Of course, that means it would also probably be weird and full of monster goons."

"Me, a Guardian?" Snow White blushed and looked away. "Oh, I don't think that that could ever happen. You're all so talented, and I'm just . . . me."

"We're all 'just me' until we choose to become something extraordinary."

At that, she felt a wistful little wisp of hope. "We'll see" was all she could say.

"Sulley!" someone called. "Snow?"

"I think that's Tiana!" Snow White said, perking up.

Whump.

Stitch landed on the ground in front of them, having dropped out of the trees. He took one look at Sulley, sniffed politely, and fell over in a swoon while making a gagging sound.

"See?" Snow White said. "The rose soap will work wonders, I promise."

"Come on," Stitch said, expanding until he was even bigger than Sulley. Glowing with energy, he parted two of the trees like they were wimpy little flower stems. "Hurry."

"What's wrong?" Sulley asked as he followed Snow White and Stitch.

"Animals need help," Stitch said. He turned around, his huge eyes landing on Snow White. "Need Snow."

7

Finally Stitch pushed his way into a clearing, shrank back down to his normal size, and shook himself like a dog, sending leaves flying. Snow White felt like sagging with relief at being reunited with the group, but she didn't want to look anything other than competent and calm. There were Tiana and Hades, but Rapunzel . . .

Well, she was all tangled up.

Or at least her hair was, wrapped around the mutant squirrels, holding them captive as they squirmed and squeaked and dripped bright green poison from their bristling barb-tipped tails.

"Oh, Snow! Thank goodness!" Rapunzel squeaked.

"Why, what can I do?" Snow White asked, confused.

"It's your forest, and you know these creatures best." Tiana neared one of the squirrels, and its sharpened buckteeth nearly snapped down on her arm. "We can't get close to them, but we thought you might be able to calm them and help figure out what kind of potion might cure whatever's infected them."

These squirrels were nothing like the darling little bright-eyed, bushy-tailed fuzz balls Snow White was used to, but she knew that somewhere inside, her animal friends remained. She approached the nearest squirrel and said, sweetly and soothingly, "Oh, you poor thing! This is just awful, what's happened to you. Wouldn't you like to feel better?"

The squirrel squeaked threateningly and gnashed its teeth, but not quite so ferociously as it had with Tiana. Trying to keep her hand from shaking, Snow White reached for its back, where it couldn't bite or scratch her. As her hand came down on the not-so-soft-now fur, the giant squirrel seemed to calm a little, releasing tension. It sighed, chittering its teeth sadly. Looking closely at its face, Snow White said, "His eyes are glowing green. But isn't the Fractured Magic purple?"

"Maybe squirrels are color-blind," Rapunzel joked from where she lay on the ground nearby while her prehensile hair did the work.

"I'd noticed that—the green." Tiana walked up to join Snow White, whose rhythmic pats and calm voice had put the squirrel in something like a trance. Its friends had quieted down, too. "Like Rapunzel said earlier, this doesn't seem like Fractured Magic. More like . . ." She bent down and lifted the squirrel's eyelid to show its bright green eye. "More like poison."

"Poison?" Snow White asked.

"Poison: a substance that is capable of causing illness or death in a living creature," Hades recited. "In case you were unfamiliar. I—I mean, *my minions*—have dabbled in poisons now and again. But not now. Now I'm a good guy."

Rapunzel raised a doubtful eyebrow at him. "I bet. So, Snow, who in this world has access to poison?"

Snow White sighed, her shoulders slumping. "Any time anything terrible happens here, I just assume it's the evil queen."

"So she has the Fractured Mirror *and* dark magic of her own. She sounds like a real treat." Tiana patted her bag. "Poison at least I can deal with. Rapunzel, can you keep watch on these critters while I brew something up?"

Rapunzel grinned. "Oh, sure. I can do this all day. They got all nice and limp when Snow showed up. She's like the squirrel whisperer!"

Snow White continued petting the squirrel, hoping it could feel her genuine care and worry for it, and that it knew it wasn't alone. If poison had turned her usual furry friends into these monstrosities, then surely the poor squirrel didn't mean to be so scary and cruel.

"You're going to be fine," she told it. "Don't worry a bit. Tiana knows just what to do."

With a firm nod, Tiana began pulling ingredients out of her bag, which looked small but seemed like it was much, much bigger on the inside.

"So how'd you get to be so good with monsters?" Sulley asked. "Most of the humans I've encountered start off being terrified. And screams have their uses, don't get me wrong, but it's pretty brave, the way you just walked right up to it."

"Oh, it's not his fault." She scratched the mutant squirrel behind the ears, and it made a contented rumbling noise. "You know, some time ago, my stepmother, the Queen . . . well, she decided she wanted me gone.

Not that life in the castle was particularly nice. I had to do all the cleaning, and I only got to eat scraps, and it was just horrid. She sent me away with her huntsman, and he seemed very cold and cruel. But once we were deep in these very woods, he broke down crying. He just couldn't do it. He couldn't hurt me."

She looked down at the red jewel right over her heart. "That poor huntsman. He sent me away, and I ran into the forest, and it was ever so frightening. Not even like you see it now, with the Fractured Magic making it truly dangerous. Back then, it was dangerous in its own way. Why, the tree branches felt like claws, and the owls living in hollow old trees seemed like vengeful ghosts, and I just broke down on the ground. I'd never felt so hopeless in all my life. And do you know what?"

"Let me guess. Something syrupy sweet and wonderful!" Hades said, batting his eyelashes and smiling beatifically, which did not suit him at all.

"Yes, actually, it *was* wonderful. Once I looked more closely at the forest, I was able to see its beauty. That's when I met the animals. When I stopped shrieking and crying, they all came out to say hello. It was as if we could understand each other, and they helped me. I told them I needed a place to sleep, and they took me right to the home of my seven friends. Since then, I come visit them every day in the forest. Inside of this squirrel—"

"Are probably seven mice, three rocks, and someone's finger?" Hades butted in.

"You know, it's very rude to interrupt," Snow White told him. There were limits to even her patience, she was learning.

"Yeah, that's not going to stop him," Rapunzel said. "Tiana, you close to done? My hair's getting knotted."

Tiana turned around, holding a bottle of swirling pink potion. With a determined "Here we go," she poured a few drops on the squirrel Snow White had lulled to sleep. Its eyes opened with a start, and it made a surprised squeak as it began to shrink. It soon returned to its normal size and fell out of Rapunzel's hair, which sagged in relief. Snow White caught the animal deftly, smoothing its fur back down.

"See? I told you. Back to normal and as handsome as ever." She scratched under its chin, and the squirrel licked her and ran up her arm to perch on her shoulder.

"Eat?" Stitch asked hopefully.

The squirrel burrowed under Snow White's hair and scolded the blue alien angrily as Snow White told Stitch, "Absolutely not!"

Stitch sighed sadly and did a handstand, sticking out his tongue at her.

Tiana was already on to the next squirrel. It only took a few drops of her potion, and each creature shrank back down to its normal size, its eyes going from a glowing poisonous green to the usual bright, warm brown and the barb on its tail falling off and shriveling away to nothing. Snow White went to each squirrel in turn, catching it as it shrank and telling it how handsome and clever it was. It was as if the squirrels had forgotten they'd ever been gigantic, vicious, and in possession of poisoned scorpion tails. They skittered up and down Snow White's legs and arms, squeaking excitedly and harmlessly flicking their tails. Soon they were all back to normal, and Rapunzel was fluffing her hair where they'd tangled bits of it up with their thrashing.

"You don't think they hid any nuts in there, do you?" she asked. "I guess I'll find out on wash day."

"Where to, now that we're not being chased?" Sulley asked, looking around the clearing.

"Well, I thought we should stop by the cottage," Snow White said. "We need food and sleep, and there are plenty of beds there." She looked Sulley up and down. "We'll have to shove some beds together for you, but there are extra pillows. And I did promise Stitch some stew."

"Stew!" Stitch shouted, sniffing the air as if hunting for a scent to follow.

"Lead the way, then," Tiana said.

But Snow White could only look around the surrounding trees with a sense of helplessness; she couldn't help feeling like she was letting everyone down. "I don't know that I can. As I told Mickey, the paths through the forest keep changing. They're more tangled than ever. And when we ran into the trees, I got all turned around. Nothing here looks like it should. It's not familiar at all. I don't know how to get to the cottage. It's a terrible feeling, being lost in your own home."

The squirrel on her shoulder—the first one that had been changed back to normal—chittered to a squirrel on the ground, and that squirrel chittered to another squirrel, all in a line. The last squirrel skittered into the bushes.

"Do the animals here talk?" Tiana asked. "Because those squirrels are up to something."

"Oh, no," Snow White said. "They can't talk. But they can understand."

After a few moments, the bushes rustled, and out stepped a grand stag, then a doe and the little fawn with its broken leg in a splint. The clouds broke and the full moon shone down on the stag's noble antlers, making them seem to glow from within. Three rabbits hopped out after deer, two turtles ambled into the clearing, and a whole flock of songbirds descended like a cloud of confetti to sing and flutter around Snow White's head. The fawn bumped her leg with its nose, and the stag stepped onto a path that she would've sworn hadn't been there just moments ago.

"I think they know the way," Snow White said, smiling. "They'll take us to the cottage again, the dear things!"

The stag led them, and the animals frolicked around Snow White as she accompanied the family of deer through a narrow moonlit path that seemed to form the moment the stag set down his hoof. The Guardians followed, and Snow White was fairly certain she heard Tiana murmur, "This is some kind of magic."

The forest was still dark and twisty, still shivering with midnight mystery, still veined with gleaming cracks of violet, but the animals lit the way, their bright eyes reflecting the moonlight. Rapunzel had to stop once and force Stitch to spit out a bluebird, but otherwise their journey was calm and unhindered. Even Hades didn't have a single word of criticism, but that might've been because snakes kept gathering lovingly around his ankles and it took a lot of concentration not to trip.

Finally the trees opened up to reveal the familiar sleeping silhouette of sloping thatch and cheerfully glowing windows. Snow White's heart beat faster when she thought perhaps her real friends from the cottage had finally returned home, but then she remembered that she had lit all those candles herself, just a few hours earlier, for all that it felt like several lifetimes had passed since she'd last stood there.

"This is it," she said. "This is the cottage." She turned to the stag and slung an arm around his smooth neck, putting her cheek against his. "Oh, thank you!"

The stag stepped back and inclined his head in a bow, then walked sedately into the forest. The doe nudged Snow White with her wet black nose, the fawn headbutted her, the birds sang sweetly in a circle around her head, and then the animals disappeared into the undergrowth, taking the moonlight with them. Once she'd finished waving goodbye, Snow White opened the door to the cottage, pickaxe in hand as she checked every corner for more enemies. How terrible it would've been to invite her new friends into her home, only for them to be attacked!

Fortunately, everything was just as it should've been—well, no. It was, of course, just as she'd left it. The house *should've* been tidy, but the fight had sent crockery and dirty spoons flying.

"It's usually nicer than this," Snow White admitted.

"Fighting seven Fractured will do a number on your home decorating," Tiana said wryly. "I see a roof and four walls, and that's good enough for me."

"Stitch smell stew," Stitch agreed. "Enough!" Then he eyed Sulley suspiciously. "Maybe enough."

Snow White laughed and leaned her pickaxe against the wall before going to check the cauldron hanging over the fire. Thankfully, the hearty stew was bubbling and fragrant. Dopey, Happy, Grumpy, Sleepy, Sneezy, Doc, and Bashful had such immense appetites that she'd made enough to feed an army. She hoped it would be enough to feed Sulley and Stitch.

She put rolls to warm by the fire, pulled potatoes out of the coals with tongs, and did her best to keep her beautiful new clothes from getting singed or covered in ash. Without being asked, Tiana began setting the table, while Rapunzel used her hair to manipulate the broom and dustpan and sweep up the broken crockery. Stitch slurped up all the water that had slopped across the floor in the fight, and Sulley set all the furniture upright before trying to sit in a chair, which collapsed.

"Uh, sorry about that," he said sheepishly. "Need more firewood?"

Hades took a chair leg out of Sulley's hand and lit it on fire with his hair. "Forget firewood. It's a torch. I don't trust moonlight that only obeys deer. It's weird."

Soon they all sat around the table—with Sulley cross-legged on the ground—laughing as they enjoyed Snow White's stew. Tiana just had to know the recipe, and they got into a deep conversation about growing herbs in the garden. Rapunzel kept swiping more dinner rolls and stuffing them into her cheeks like a chipmunk, and Stitch made himself slightly bigger so he could hold more food. Sulley fumbled with one of the small spoons, blowing on his stew before daintily slurping it. Hades didn't eat, apparently, so instead he focused on trying to get someone to pull his finger, which everyone staunchly refused to do.

All in all, it was one of the nicest meals of Snow White's life, even though it was eaten at midnight, surrounded by a rapidly deteriorating forest and the promise of a treacherous journey to come. As the others cleaned up, she trudged upstairs to set the beds to rights. They were all mussed from the Fractured. She pushed several beds together for Sulley, fluffed all the pillows, and turned back the covers just so.

Everyone came upstairs, and Hades made a beeline for the bed marked with Grumpy's name, muttering, "I get this guy."

Once her new friends were comfortable, Snow White went gladly to her own bed, grateful for a quiet moment to absorb all that had happened. To think: in just one night, she'd gone from her normal life to learning that not only did magic exist, but there were other worlds! She'd never dreamed the universe might be so big, or that she herself could have a starring role in it. She fell asleep with her giant pickaxe leaning against the wall and a smile on her face. Sure, they had a harrowing quest ahead of them, and yes, Happy, Doc, Sleepy, Bashful, Sneezy, Grumpy, and Dopey were surely in trouble. But she had new friends, she wasn't alone, and she was starting to learn that she had her own skills that could help others in need.

She slept deeply, exhausted by the day's events. All was well, right up until sometime around midnight, when the door downstairs opened with a sinister creak.

———◇———

8

Snow White startled awake in the darkness, every sense on alert. What had pulled her from her dreams? Was it a noise? A smell? There was no smoke. Nothing moved in the room.

Except . . .

She squinted as her eyes adjusted, hunting for something unexpected in the shadows.

There. Was that . . . was her hairbrush . . . glowing purple?

Before she could call out, the brush flew across the room and smacked her right between the eyes. Lightning bloomed in her vision, blinding her, her head aching.

"What—why?" she sputtered, her hands hunting around the bed for the rogue brush and finding nothing.

Smack!

It struck her right across the cheek this time, hard as a slap.

"Tiana!" she shouted. "Sulley! Rap—"

Before she could finish Rapunzel's name, she got rapped—across the nose with her own hairbrush. Her whole face stinging, she fell flat back against her pillow, pulled the blanket over her head, and rolled out from under the covers and off the bed. She landed on the floorboards in a crouch and reached for her pickaxe.

"Help!" she shouted before the brush could hit her again. This time, she tried to swat it away, but it crunched into her hair, twisting into a tangle and yanking, hard. Snow White yelped and grabbed for the brush, but it bucked in her hand, twisting harder. She felt hairs being yanked out, *pop pop pop*, and dropped her pickaxe and grabbed the brush with both hands, holding it still as it trembled, trying to fly free.

Tiana called, "Snow, what's wrong?"

"Fractured Magic!" she yelped as the brush tried to yank every hair on her head out by its roots.

"Where?" Tiana asked, followed by "Ouch! Is that a fork?"

"Ariel calls that a dinglehopper," Hades added helpfully from somewhere in the hallway outside. "I call it a pain in my—Hey! Ow! How many forks are there in this cottage, anyway? Seven adjective names plus one weather name equals—Ouch!"

"Hey, what's going on?" Sulley asked from a pile of blankets before screeching, leaping out of his nest, and running away from a large pair of tongs.

Stitch had his claws sunken into the ceiling and was skittering around, trying to avoid an aggressive ladle as he screeched, "No soup! No soup!"

Rapunzel's hair formed a protective cage around her as she tried to sneak out of the room, followed by a swarm of furious saucepans that seemed to take umbrage at her cast-iron frying pan.

Snow White finally managed to yank out the brush, and it jerked and bucked in her hands as she stood and staggered over to her vanity table. She opened a drawer with one foot and hurled the brush inside on top of her winter cloak, then slammed the drawer before the brush could escape. Unsure how to keep it trapped, she pulled a long scarf out of her top drawer and used it to tie the drawer shut. It rattled and banged as the brush tried to fight its way out, and she grabbed her pickaxe and ran for the stairs.

On the landing, Tiana and Hades fought against forks—flying forks with a familiar purple glow.

"You guys?" Sulley called from downstairs. "I could use a little help."

"What now?" Tiana called, trying in vain to pluck a stabby purple fork from the air.

"I've never fought a Fractured cottage before!" Sulley shouted. "The cauldron is—"

A resounding *bong* echoed through the house.

"Angry," Sulley finished, sounding dizzy and stunned.

Tiana slapped a fork to the ground and darted downstairs. Hades followed, a twisted and burnt fork clutched in his fist. Snow White skidded down the top steps. As the purple-threaded rug runner yanked itself straight, she tripped and fell down the remaining stairs, dropping her pickaxe and barely managing to do a somersault and land on her feet in the kitchen, catching the weapon neatly, much to her own surprise.

The sight that met her eyes would've been hilarious if she hadn't known about the evil Fractured Magic that

lit the dark room with a malevolent purple phospho-
rescence. Sulley was covered in brown gravy, sparring
with her stew cauldron, which was a lot more nimble
than it looked. Tiana ducked as plates riddled with
purple cracks launched themselves from the drying rack
directly at her head. Hades threatened the tablecloth
with fists wreathed in fire as the once neatly folded
fabric flapped at him like a cape beckoning a bull to a
fight.

Snow White heard a howl behind her and ducked as
Stitch launched himself down the stairs. Rapunzel followed, sliding down the tautly pulled runner like she
was surfing on a sled. Snow White and the Guardians
regrouped in the center of the kitchen, readying their
weapons and preparing for the next onslaught of dark
magic. The forks and spoons and chairs and plates all
paused in midair, their violet cracks pulsating like a
heartbeat.

"Are we gonna fight or what?" Hades asked, sounding like he would be disappointed if the answer was no.

In response, the door slammed open, bouncing
against the wall. The Fractured goon that appeared—
a portly alligator with a staff—barely fit through, its
massive shoulders squeezing until it stood inside the

cottage. Four more goons followed it within and stood in a row, their crackling energy filling the room with enough electricity to raise the hair on the back of Snow White's neck. She spotted a vulture with a halberd, a boar with a sword, an eagle with a bow and arrows, and a goblinesque bat creature with an axe, all their faces twisted with cruel intent. With the candles out and the fire gone cold, the only light was their ominous violet glow. She held her pickaxe, wishing she'd had more time to practice with her weapon or at least ask the others for pointers.

"What do we do?" she asked.

"You know what we do," Tiana responded. "We take down these Fractured goons!"

Snow White was worried about the lack of light, and she thought of asking Hades to use his blue flames to light the candles . . . but then she remembered that the household goods were not currently on their side and that fire could cause even more harm than the goons.

"Do we start now?" Hades asked. "Or are we waiting for something? A formal invitation? No? Good." He reared up and threw a fireball at the alligator, knocking it backward in a burst of light.

As if that strike had offered permission, the fight broke out in earnest. Tiana and Hades paired up to fight the big alligator, while Sulley, Rapunzel, and Stitch set their sights on three of the backup goons. For a moment, Snow White just stared at the last goon, the bat-thing, but then it sneered and ran at her, swinging its axe, and she hefted her pickaxe and leapt forward. Her brain had a tiny thought, just for a moment—

What am I doing? I don't know how to fight!

But then her body answered that thought with an assertive slash that knocked the goon back into a chair. The chair seemed to take that personally; it pulsated with purple light as it bolted upright and skittered toward Snow White like a spider.

"I'm so sorry!" she yelped as she slashed at it with her pickaxe. It was Happy's chair, and it exploded the moment her pickaxe struck it, the pieces flying across the room in a very unhappy manner.

The goon was back up, and Snow White focused on evading its slashes and hitting it with everything she had. Something in her didn't want to use her full force, wanted to be careful and gentle and hold back. But another part of her, a new part, pressed bravely forward, taking control of her hands and jerking her body out of range of her enemy's strikes as if she'd been doing it all her life. She was gaining confidence, understanding how best to swing her pickaxe, when the goon darted forward and swung its own axe—right into her hip. The pain was startling, white hot and burning, and she wanted to run away crying, and yet she also wanted to scream with every ounce of breath in her lungs, and that part won out.

With a mighty roar, she did a flying leap, her pickaxe arcing down hard enough to destroy the goon. It exploded in a cascade of purple sparks, and Snow White leaned against the wall, afraid to reach down and see how much damage the axe had done to her hip.

"Snow's hit," Hades shouted, and Tiana nodded and ducked out of the fight, leaving him to face the biggest goon alone as the battle raged all around the kitchen.

Mugs flew across the room, exploding against Tiana's back as she ran to Snow White's side.

"Where'd it get you?" she asked, and when Snow White showed her, Tiana gasped. "Yeah, they hit hard. Hold on. I've got the potion ready." She held out a glass tube filled with vermilion liquid, and Snow White considered it for a moment, remembering something she'd almost forgotten about eating and drinking things that didn't seem quite right. "It's a healing potion," Tiana said. "I've got to get back in there. These big goons are dangerous."

As Tiana threw herself back into the fray, Snow White popped the cork out of the potion and drank it, noting that it tasted like fresh strawberries and sunshine. Much like whatever Mickey had done, it was as if the wound just disappeared, a warmth spreading through her body and making her feel stronger and ready to fight again. She wasn't sure what to do with the empty tube, and in the split second that she thought about it, the broom beside her rose into the air, crackling with purple energy, and swung at her head.

"That's very rude! No wonder Mickey didn't trust you," Snow White said, tossing the glass aside and taking up her pickaxe. It wasn't the best weapon for facing off with a broom, and the dratted thing kept rapping her knuckles as she struggled to fight it off. The dust bucket joined its partner and flew into the air, landing on her head and leaving her in darkness.

"Maybe I don't particularly enjoy sweeping, but that's quite enough!" She reached up, yanked the bucket off her head, and took hold of the handle, which she swung in a circle to knock the broom aside. Once she'd flung the bucket across the room, she dove under the table, hoping that perhaps she'd be less noticeable if she stayed out of the way.

Two more of the Fractured goons were gone, and as she watched, Rapunzel finished hers off with what appeared to be a gout of flame burning around her frying pan.

"And that's my favorite recipe," Rapunzel said, expertly spinning the pan in her hand.

The only goon left now was the big one, and although Tiana and Hades were getting in plenty of good hits, it just wasn't going down as easily as its compatriots. Rapunzel, Sulley, and Stitch surrounded it, leaving it trapped by all five of Snow White's companions. She wondered if she should get out from under the table to help, but it wasn't a large kitchen, after all, and her new friends seemed competent and accustomed to working together as a team. If she got involved, she'd probably just get in the way or slow them down.

Forks and spoons and cups were still flying through the air, battering her friends as they focused their energy on the last goon standing. There was so much motion everywhere that it was like a swarm of flies, and with only her huge pickaxe as a weapon, there was little Snow White could do on that front, either. Still, her friends were landing solid hits, working in tandem—

Whack!

The cauldron smacked into Sulley's chest, knocking him down and pinning him to the ground.

Whump!

Snow White's skillet clocked Rapunzel from the back, and Rapunzel's frying pan flew out of her hand as she slumped to the ground.

Smack!

A jug broke over Hades's head, dousing his flaming hair in a puff of smoke. He seemed to go limp as he felt around his head, muttering, "I'm too young to go bald. Honestly. I'm not even ready to buy a convertible chariot."

Now it was just Tiana and Stitch fighting the last goon, and then every fork and knife flew at Tiana, pinning her to the wall by her coat. Only Stitch was left, and when the washtub landed on his head, trying to press him to the ground like a turtle shell, he did the strangest thing.

He started shaking, his whole body glowing orange like he was on fire, and then he began to grow. He'd started as tall as the table, but then he was as tall as

Hades, and then as tall as the Fractured goon, and then his head scraped against the ceiling.

"Don't hurt friends!" he howled, rearing back to punch the goon with a fist wreathed in flames. The goon flew back, hit the wall, and slid down . . . but it wasn't done yet.

Swinging its staff, the goon stupidly advanced, facing off with the now-larger alien. Stitch's antennae quivered, all four of his hands in fists, his mouth open to show rows of teeth. The goon tried to swing its weapon, but Stitch kept growing, now crouched over, his fist as big as the monstrous alligator. Grabbing the goon, Stitch screamed at it, spit flying everywhere. The goon didn't cry or whimper or beg or squirm; it just mindlessly lashed out with its weapon like it hadn't quite gotten word that it was doomed.

As Stitch grew bigger and bigger, the silverware flying around had nowhere to go and fell to the floor. He finally knocked into the table she was hiding under, and Snow White had to scramble back as his mass shoved it across the wooden boards, legs scraping. The ceiling squealed, the boards buckling as Stitch expanded, and Snow White got a horrible sinking feeling.

"Stitch, you have to stop growing!" she called. "You'll destroy the cottage!"

Stitch looked for her, the goon still in one giant paw. "Yes, destroy!" he agreed, nodding his head with enough force to send bits of plaster raining down from the ceiling.

"No destroy!" she shouted back. "This is my home. My friends are the closest thing I have to a family. If you destroy it, we'll have no place to live!"

Stitch stopped growing, thinking hard. "Family," he murmured. "'Ohana. 'Ohana means family. And family means—"

"Not destroying someone's house!" Hades shouted in agreement. "At least, in most families. In my family, we destroy everyone's everything, but that's just us. That's just Olympus. We're quirky like that. So focus on that little goon in your hand. You want to destroy? Destroy that."

"Yes, destroy," Stitch said softly to himself. He refocused on the goon and squeezed until it exploded in a shower of sparks.

The moment the goon was gone, the purple light in the house fizzled out, and all the previously enchanted home goods that still had room to maneuver fell to the floor with a crash that made Snow White wince. The only light now was the orange glow around Stitch, who was taking up most of the space. With one exhale, his skin dimmed back to its usual shade of blue, and the temperature dropped, leaving them all in the dark.

"It's okay now," Snow White said. "You can shrink back."

But Stitch looked at her with big troubled eyes that glimmered in the darkness.

"Can't," he said.

———————◇———————

9

Stitch understood his molecular structure, knew everything about the difference between solid and liquid and gas and how the entire world—every world—was shaped by the space between atoms. But knowing and doing were two different things. He'd never grown this big before, never stretched himself to his limits.

And now his body didn't want to go back.

The goon was gone, and Stitch's friends were safe. No more annoying kitchen things were flying around like purple mosquitoes. There was no more need to fight, no need to be angry. Yet when the anger drained away, Stitch found something new.

Fear.

He'd always worried that maybe one day his powers just wouldn't work properly and the Guardians wouldn't need him anymore and he'd be left behind. Like if he were stuck in the wrong shape or size, maybe trapped as a gas, insubstantial and spread out. *Do gas molecules forget how to be solid?* he wondered. It was certainly easier to turn water into ice than gas into water. This felt like a puzzle he couldn't quite solve, something like the colorful cube his friend Lilo had once handed him back home when he'd been too fidgety while she was trying to do her homework. She'd shown him how to turn the little squares this way and that, how he should try to twist all the red squares to one side, the blue squares to another. The toy had frustrated him, and he'd chewed on it for a moment in rage before swallowing it, thinking that his stomach acid would sort it out just fine. That would teach the cube to defy him!

Lilo had held out her hand, though, and he'd horked it back up. When it landed in her palm, covered in saliva, she'd told him that even if his behavior was better, his spit levels were reaching dangerous new heights.

But there was no annoying puzzle cube here. The building blocks in question were part of his own body, and they liked where they were, thank you very much.

"Having a little trouble breathing here," Sulley said, currently an uncomfortable lump under Stitch's rear end. "Also, not the best place to be stuck, no offense."

"Yeah, this is not the most comfortable position," Rapunzel said from somewhere between Stitch's ribs and the wall, her voice muffled. "I feel like I'm being crushed by friendship."

"At least you're not near the slobber puddle," Hades added. "I'm having enough trouble getting the fire rekindled, you know?" With a slight fizzing sound, the room began to glow ever so slightly blue. "There. That's better."

Stitch closed his mouth and swallowed back the tide of saliva. Hopefully, that fire would keep burning without his constant, fearful drooling; the dark was not friendly.

His head drooped until his nose touched the floor. Everyone else needed just one thing right now: for him to be small again. But he couldn't get there, couldn't remember how to do it. For all that everyone else thought him a simple creature, his mind could move at the speed of light, and he understood physics better than any of them. They couldn't help him. They didn't know how.

Someone was crawling under his armpit, and he

sucked in a breath to help them escape his bulk. It was Snow White, dragging herself out from under a nearby table. He liked Snow. She was kind and soft and smelled like flowers and food. She crawled over to his head and put a small hand against his big blue nose.

"You can't change back?" she asked him calmly.

"Stitch can't . . . remember . . ." He sighed sadly, antennae drooping.

"Well, think about what it feels like to be smaller." She rubbed his nose, and he blinked and perked up the tiniest bit. That was a very nice feeling. "Think about how you see the world when you're your regular size. How the grass feels under your feet. Think about how tiny you feel when you look up at the stars. Remember how it feels when a fresh cinnamon bun fits exactly in your mouth."

Stitch licked his chops.

"To be fair, he can probably fit four of those things in his mouth, even when he's not gigantic," Hades commented. "I saw him yawn once, and it was like looking into Charybdis. But don't tell Charybdis I said that."

Snow White grabbed Stitch's nose to help him focus on something besides the thought of cinnamon buns and biting Hades. "Think about what it feels like to hug your family and notice that you're just the right size to fit. Think about how nice it is to curl up in your own special bed. Think about how the world looks when you're precisely as tall as the table. Isn't it nice, to be exactly who you are?"

Stitch blinked thoughtfully. "Doughnuts," he muttered. "Lilo hug."

He could remember. He could remember very well.

"That's right," Snow White encouraged him. "Tell me what you love."

Stitch stuck his tongue in his nose and cocked his head. "Luau. Ice cream. Elvis."

He closed his eyes and exhaled, flooded with good memories, and then he was just a little bit smaller. Around the room, the others groaned and pulled themselves away from the wall or up from the floor.

"Keep going." Snow White reached for his gigantic hand. "Think of the things you love, and they'll remind you who you are."

"Guardians," he whispered. "Magic. Friends."

With each calm exhale, Stitch shrank. He could feel his atoms remembering exactly how to be Stitch-sized. Bit by bit, he was as tall as the room, and then the door, and then, finally, the table. When he was exactly the right size, he opened his eyes and blinked curiously.

"Stitch remembered," he said, relieved. Then,

squeezing Snow White's hand, he added, "Thank you, friend."

Snow White sighed with relief—because she could breathe again. The rest of the team walked up, brushing blue fur off their outfits and fussing with their hair. Sulley had a purple bruise sticking up like a small hill on his head, and Rapunzel was dragging one of her feet a bit.

"I know just what y'all need." Tiana reached into her bag. She pulled out several of the glass tubes of healing potion and passed them around. Everyone who needed one drank and handed the tube back. "Gonna need some new ingredients soon," Tiana muttered to herself. "We're taking plenty of knocks around here."

"What kind of ingredients?" Snow White asked, since it was her world and she wanted to be helpful.

"Gemstones, certain plants, fruits," Tiana said.

"Oh! You're welcome to look through my garden around back for any plants that might help. And the mine isn't too far away. My friends always find plenty of gems." Her shoulders slumped. "I still can't believe they're gone."

"Find family soon," Stitch said, patting her hand.

Sulley yawned, giant jaw cracking. "Soon, meaning after a few more hours of sleep, right? Because I scare best on a solid eight hours."

Rapunzel pushed the curtain aside and gazed out into the night. "We do need sleep, but whoever sent those Fractured goons knows where we are. We need to leave. We're sitting ducklings."

"Not necessarily." Tiana tapped her fingers as she thought. "I don't think this Queen is the type to try the same thing twice. She seems like she's all about the drama."

"Oh, yes, that definitely describes her!" Snow White agreed. "I do think that if she were going to try such a thing, the next wave of magic would already be upon us. She's likely got something else planned, something unexpected. She can be patient when it suits her."

"So we take turns keeping an eye out until morning." Tiana stifled a yawn. "I'll take first watch. You guys go sleep."

"*Pfft.* Sleep. So overrated. Just like mortality." In a swirl of smoke, Hades stepped forward, his hair now back to a brightly blazing blue. "I don't need sleep. You all go do the open-mouth-snoring-drooling thing, and I'll sit here and be just as bored as I would be in a cramped little bed irrationally titled 'Happy.'"

"But you were in Grumpy's bed," Snow White reminded him.

Hades shrugged. "Pretty sure that one got smashed in the fork fight, or at least covered in monster dandruff. Might as well rename it Sad."

"I'm not sure we can trust him," Sulley said.

"I can hear you," Hades muttered. "You're not even trying to hide it."

"We have to trust him." Snow White stuck her chin out. "He's one of us. Mickey said so."

Tiana and Rapunzel shared a glance, and Snow White, knowing that they didn't necessarily agree with her, felt her spirits fall. Hades picked up an overturned chair, zapped the kitchen fire back to life, and sat beside it, one foot on his knee.

"You guys got any books around here?" he asked. "*The Iliad*? *The Odyssey*? Something new and hot?"

"I have some bedtime stories that I read to fall asleep—" Snow White began.

Hades made a polite gagging sound. "No thanks. Those sound like the kind of rag in which everyone lives happily ever after. Disgusting. Guess I'll just work on my memoir." He pulled a scroll and quill out of his robes and began scribbling.

With Hades settled in, Snow White lit a few candles

from the fire and handed them out before following the others upstairs. On the landing, Tiana, Rapunzel, and Sulley were whispering. As Snow White reached them, they broke apart.

"I'm not feeling that sleepy," Sulley said, clearly stretching the truth. "I'll probably stay awake. Just in case. Although I'll take one of those bedtime stories, if you've got one lying around. Anything with a monster in it would be great."

Snow White nodded and fetched a book—which looked tiny in Sulley's paws—that featured a wicked dragon. She appreciated the care he took in handling it as he lounged across two of the beds and began reading.

Once everyone was settled, Snow White curled back up in her own bed. She'd never felt so anxious in her own home, but, well, she'd been attacked there. Twice. It was no longer the haven it had once been, and it wouldn't be safe again until they'd found the Fractured Mirror and stopped the Queen from using it to cause mischief. It wasn't a long way to her castle—at least, not usually. Now, with the forest growing bigger, meaner, and more foreboding with every passing moment, its paths twisted and deceptive, it would likely be a longer journey than anyone wanted.

As she lay in the darkness, her mind spinning,

Snow White thought she might never close her eyes again, even with a god and a monster keeping watch. Her exhaustion was simply too much, however, and she fell into a deep and dreamless sleep.

When she woke up, sunlight fell through the windows in bright, warm beams, the birds outside singing . . . well, almost normally. There was something odd about their songs, something off, and when she got up and stretched and looked outside, she could barely see past the crowding trees and their leaves, touched here and there with purple veins.

Snow White usually got up earlier than everyone else and was accustomed to using this time to get started with her morning. Setting the cottage to rights always made her feel ready to face the day, with everything just so. Before heading downstairs to tidy up, however, she had to stop at the bedroom door and turn back to check all the beds and make sure her new friends hadn't been replaced by Fractured. Tiana and Rapunzel were asleep under their covers, soft mounds gently breathing. Stitch was turned around, his head poking out of the covers at the foot of the bed, two hands falling off the side, his mouth open and tongue slobbering onto a pool on the ground below.

Sulley, however, wasn't awake and alert like he was

supposed to be. He was snoring, strewn across two beds and surrounded by Snow White's friends from the forest. Birds nestled in his fur, rabbits were snuggled up to his sides, and a raccoon curled on his chest, her striped tail tucked under his blue-and-purple chin. Their tiny, squeaky snores were an adorable counterpoint to his deep growling ones.

Smiling to herself, Snow White went downstairs and beheld the wreck left behind by the most recent fight. Broken crockery and glass were all over the place, the cauldron had splattered gravy across the wall, and the washtub had spilled soapy water everywhere. With a sigh, she poked at the broom, making sure it was no longer ensorcelled, then set to sweeping up the mess.

"Need help?" Hades asked from beside the fire.

"That would be lovely!"

"Oh, I wasn't offering. I was just making conversation." He turned back to the fire. "Yeah, gods don't sweep. That's not how being a god works. We have minions for that. Can you imagine if I had to sweep the Underworld? That's all I'd do. Just endless brooms devoured by endless fires, and then I'd have to find more brooms. No thanks."

Recognizing a lost cause, Snow White went back to

sweeping. Once the floor was no longer dangerous for bare feet, she looked through the cupboard and began making pancakes. As soon as the food started cooking, Stitch skittered down the stairs, pulled a chair up to the table, tied a napkin around his neck, and collected a fork and knife to hold in two of his fists.

"A little help might be nice," Snow White hinted, and he sighed and set to licking the windows clean. It wasn't *exactly* what she'd meant, but it was effective.

Tiana and Rapunzel wandered downstairs together, yawning. Tiana offered to whip up some eggs, and Rapunzel began setting the table. Sulley appeared a few moments later, scratching his belly and somehow ignoring the fact that three songbirds were nesting in the fur on his shoulders. Daintily using his claws, he took up a messy pile of napkins and tea towels and started folding.

It was nice having something close to a normal breakfast with the Guardians. Sure, she was worried about her missing friends, but after seeing the Guardians fight, she had full faith that they had the skill, determination, and teamwork necessary to perform an effective rescue mission. When the food was gone—Snow White was fairly certain there would never be leftovers with this crew—everyone (except Hades) offered to help tidy up. Snow White wasn't sure how to respond to Stitch's offer to lick the dishes clean, but Tiana took him along as she looked through the garden outside for herbs or flowers that might be helpful in her potions. Rapunzel actually seemed to enjoy putting the kitchen to rights, and even offered to paint a mural sometime, when the danger was past.

"So you're sure we'll be able to save this world?" Snow White asked.

"Definitely!" Rapunzel made a frame with her fingers and looked at the empty white wall through one eye. "That's kind of what we do. For the wall, I'm thinking a big tree full of all the animals, with flowers around the outside. No purple cracks allowed. Right?"

"Flames," Hades said from where he sat with his legs kicked up on the table. "Definitely go for flames."

Once Sulley had pushed all the remaining beds back into place upstairs and Snow White had tucked all the covers in just so, there was nothing left to do. The cottage was neat as a pin, just the way Snow White liked it, and she could imagine Happy, Doc, Bashful, Sleepy, Sneezy, Grumpy, and Dopey coming home, pleased to find everything ready and comfortable. The place had been a wreck when she first found it, but they'd all developed a rhythm, and it made her smile to think things might go back to normal someday.

Well, somewhat normal. Perhaps the Fractured Mirror could be found and destroyed, but the Stellar Magic, as she understood it, was now part of her world forever. That meant that even if the purple cracks receded and the goons were no longer a threat, she herself would still be . . . changed. Things would be different no matter what.

But that was fine. Change, so far, had been good to her. Her time with the Queen had been wretched, and she'd been driven away from everything she'd ever known and loved . . . but then she'd found her seven friends and a life free of cruelty and suffering. Perhaps this change, too, would bring new joys.

Once the fire was out and all the candles had been snuffed, she grabbed her pickaxe, closed the door behind the Guardians, and turned to the path that led to the mine. It was still there, thankfully, although the forest really did seem bigger and darker and wilder, the trees and leaves shot through with worrisome purple cracks.

"It's not too far," she said. "Why, Happy, Sneezy, Sleepy, Dopey, Doc, Grumpy, and Bashful go this way every day. Tiana can find the jewels she might need, and then we'll be right off to the Queen's castle."

"Will you, now?" said a new voice—a deep and sinister voice.

Out of the forest's shadows stepped someone Snow White had hoped to never see again.

The evil queen's huntsman.

———◇———

10

The Snow White of old might've turn and fled. But now she immediately went into a defensive position, her pickaxe at the ready. She didn't have to look behind her to know that the Guardians were likewise in position to fight.

"What do you want?" she asked.

"The same thing I wanted last time and was denied," the Huntsman replied in a strange, dull monotone. "The heart of Snow White."

He lunged forward with his hunting knife, but Snow White easily parried it with her pickaxe. He slashed down again, and she caught his blade against her own.

Although he was significantly taller and had more mass, she was pleased to find she had enough strength to hold him off. He pressed down harder, trying to force his knife toward her throat, and she looked up into his eyes. When they'd last parted in the forest, when he'd decided not to kill her and had told her to run away and never come back, his eyes had been the color of summer grass in the sun. Now they were an entirely different green altogether—acid, poisonous, glowing.

Just like the mutated squirrels.

"Don't hurt him!" she called to her friends. "He's been poisoned!"

The Huntsman yanked his knife away and went into a crouch, his glowing green eyes twitching madly as the Guardians advanced.

"You cannot best her," he said in that strange ensorcelled voice. "She will take her due, as she wishes."

"Grab him!" Tiana shouted, and Stitch howled and launched himself at the Huntsman's legs.

The Huntsman was so focused on Snow White that he wasn't prepared to be knocked over by a tumbling cannonball of blue alien, and he fell to the ground with a grunt, his knife skittering across the dirt path. Before he could get up, Sulley leapt over and put a huge hand down on his chest, pinning him in place.

"Yeah, nobody's taking any due today, bud. Just stay right down there while we figure things out," Sulley said, holding the squirming man down with ease.

"Can he be cured?" Snow White asked. "He was kind to me once, and I don't think he means what he's saying."

"Oh, he means it now," Tiana replied, reaching into her bag. "But he probably won't in a minute. This poison is peculiar stuff. If I'd known we'd be fighting two kinds of dark magic, I would've brought more ingredients." She grinned. "I might need some help here, in case he doesn't want to open his mouth."

Sulley held down the Huntsman, who kicked and flailed, and Snow White pinched his nose shut so that he would open his mouth.

"I'm terribly sorry about this, but it really is for the best, you know," she muttered, even though he didn't seem to be listening. When he finally ran out of air and opened his mouth for a ragged gasp, Tiana took advantage of that desperate breath to pour one of her potions down his throat. He spluttered and thrashed, then went utterly limp. When he opened his eyes again, they no longer glowed a cruel acid green but were instead the warm, friendly summer green that Snow White remembered.

"Your Highness, forgive me!" he said, voice breaking. "Yesterday, the Queen bade me drink a green liquid most foul—I don't know why—and it filled me with confusion and strangeness. She told me to find you, to take your—" He gasped and turned his face away. "It's as if I was trapped in a nightmare, and I couldn't make myself stop."

"It wasn't your fault," Snow White said gently. "I know you didn't mean it." But then her smile turned down. "Still, you were in your right mind the last time she sent you to kill me, and yet you must've gone back to her service, knowing she was wicked and would only use you to cause harm. You must take some responsibility for that."

The Huntsman shook his head like he was trying to wake up from a bad dream. "What else is there, child? What other life for me? Some people are builders or farmers or cooks or bards, but I'm a huntsman, and I must hunt."

Snow White sighed sadly. "I don't think that's good enough. You cannot go back to the Queen again only to be sent on some other foul errand. I know there is kindness in you. I would suggest you leave her service— and this forest—forever. Find some other life that won't force you to compromise your beliefs. I once thought a person simply was who they were, incapable of change . . ." She looked to her weapon and smiled. "But I've since learned that when faced with the chance to grow and learn, we have the ability to choose a new path."

"Snow is right. There is so much more out there. Why would you want to work for someone who clearly only intends harm?" Rapunzel asked.

"Well, there is a recession," Hades said, inspecting his nails. "And the cost of living—whew! Have you seen what they want for an amphora of oil these days?"

Sulley looked to Snow White. "Should I let him go?"

Snow White considered it. "Will you go far away from here, and never speak to the Queen again, and forget you ever saw us? Find some new skill, maybe help those in need instead of harming them?"

The Huntsman stared up at her, eyes brimming with tears. "Yes, Your Highness. Yes. Thank you for your benevolence. The Queen would not be so kind."

Snow White nodded to Sulley, and he lifted his paw. The Huntsman stood and straightened his hat, then looked to where his knife lay on the path.

"Don't even think about it," Tiana said, placing her foot firmly over the blade.

The Huntsman bowed his head. "Forgive me. May

the Queen never find you." And then he slipped into the forest and was gone.

"Do you think he'll stay away?" Tiana asked. She moved her foot and looked down at the knife as if it were something particularly disgusting she'd found on the bottom of her shoe.

"Oh, yes," Snow White said. "I just hope he really will try to start over and find some better purpose."

Hades strode to where Tiana was considering the Huntsman's knife. "May I?" he asked, then, without bothering to wait for an answer, "Yes? Thanks. Good." He picked up the knife, used it to pick at his teeth, and then let his flames swarm over it, enrobing it in fire. Everything smelled like burning metal, and then he turned his hand upside down to let a pile of ash fall to the ground. "Knife problem over. Let's get on with it."

With the Huntsman gone and the way clear, Snow White had no choice but to lead on. The trail to the mine seemed to have more twists and turns than she remembered, but it must've been correct, as they passed the pretty little waterfall she remembered.

"Nice place," Tiana said, pausing to walk beside Snow White.

"It usually is." Snow White sighed. "Or it used to be. Why, even when things are normal, there's this ominous sort of feeling that hangs over me, as if the Queen is plotting something horrid. But it is pretty. Is your world much like it?"

"Not much." Tiana chuckled fondly. "It's hot where I'm from, and instead of these big old shadowy forests, we have humidity and swamps and bugs. Don't get me wrong—New Orleans is beautiful, and the city is always lively. But like this place, it can be treacherous, especially when there's somebody there who wants to cause harm."

Snow White glanced at an apple core left by the trail. She could imagine Dopey tossing it over his shoulder without a care in the world. "I just worry about my poor missing friends. I feel so helpless, knowing they're with the Queen."

"I have a best friend, too," Tiana told her. "Lottie." She snorted and shook her head. "Girl can talk a mile a minute, but she's true blue all the way. If somebody stole her, I imagine I'd move mountains to get her back. Or maybe mausoleums, since we're talking about New Orleans. Just remember—we're all here with you. And we're gonna save your friends."

"I appreciate all of you leaving your own worlds to help. I'm positive you have ever so much to do—"

"Pshaw, Snow. You'd do the same for us."

Snow White looked down at her pickaxe. "Oh, well, I would surely try."

"I know you would," Tiana said firmly. "Everybody has to start somewhere. With time and practice, you'll get stronger and more confident. The first time I led a mission, I was wobbly as that little fawn you helped. But I learned and got better. Belle helped me so much—kept my spirits up and told me I was doing fine. It helps, knowing the other Guardians have your back. So take it from me. . . ." She met Snow White's gaze, her eyes warm and genuine. "You're doing fine."

Tiana hurried up ahead to keep Stitch from falling into the river as he investigated a toad, and Snow White realized that Tiana really did have a gift. She was brave and competent, and even if she'd needed help to reach her potential, she was a natural leader. Snow White wondered if she could ever be that way herself. Not that she was anything like the Guardians—she wasn't as brave and strong as they were—but she always wanted to be of service. Still, she could feel the calluses forming where her palm gripped her pickaxe and promised herself that she would not let her new friends down.

The path wound around the mountain exactly as she remembered it, and they were able to cross the log bridge that led to the mine, although the log seemed narrower and the gorge seemed deeper and more foreboding. The mountain didn't seem quite as changed as the forest, and Snow White felt a little lift to know that some things, at least, could be counted on.

"The entrance to the mine is just after this pass," she said, pointing ahead up the well-trodden path.

If things had been normal, Happy, Doc, Sleepy, Bashful, Grumpy, Dopey, and Sneezy would've been in the mine at that very moment, the sounds of their pickaxes and songs floating down the mountain. Snow White hated the quiet without them and couldn't help wondering if the Queen had captured them in the mine, or perhaps on their way home, or even in the cottage as they washed up for supper. There was no way to know—not until she found them, saved them, and asked to hear their story.

The mine finally came into view, a gaping black maw in the mountain. Snow White looked to the vault, thinking that perhaps Tiana would find what she needed there, but the doors hung open, limp on their hinges. That vault should've been full of gems, a lifetime of wealth neatly sorted by type and clarity according to Doc's watchful eye. Instead, she saw only empty barrels and Doc's favorite loupe lying forgotten on the hard-packed dirt.

"Oh, no," she murmured. "Someone terrible has been here. There should be plenty of gems, but they've all been stolen!"

"Sounds like something a competent villain would do," Hades said, picking up the loupe and looking through it before tossing it away. "I mean, any villain that sees a vault and leaves it alone isn't much of an evil mastermind, you know?" Tiana looked at him sternly, hands on her hips, and he added, "Is how I would've thought in the past, before I saw the error of my ways and decided to . . . be good or whatever."

"There should still be plenty of gems in the mine," Snow White told Tiana. "Every time I've stepped inside, why, I've seen them glimmering all over the walls!"

"Let's hope so. I found all the herbs and flowers I need, but without certain gemstones, my potions definitely won't pack a punch. Can't make a gumbo without a roux."

Snow White led the group to the mine entrance. The yawning chasm seemed so much more threatening than she'd remembered.

"Hades, could you please provide some light?" she asked.

"Sure thing, doll. I love creepy underground places. Dependable sort of ambiance, you know? Reminds me of home." He twirled his fingers, producing a ball of bright blue flame, and led the way into the darkness.

The blue fire cast eerie shadows on the walls, and Snow White realized how much more cheerful the mine was with the warm golden light of lanterns shining at regular intervals, when her friends (except Dopey, of course) were happily singing as their pickaxes rang out with staccato clicks and the occasional chime as a gem was uncovered. She could see evidence of their time here: new tunnels just begun, the hoofprints of a deer in the dirt, one of Dopey's old, patched socks. It only made her miss them all the more.

But, oddly, she didn't see the telltale gleam of gems. As they walked deeper and deeper within the mountain, following the wood-and-metal tracks used for mining carts, a sense of foreboding settled around her. It was colder in here, cut off from the sun. Soon the light of the outside world had completely disappeared, and even when she looked back, she saw only endless darkness.

"It's not usually this . . ." She wasn't sure how to continue.

"Creepy?" Rapunzel offered.

"Dark and cold and ominous?" Tiana added.

"Cramped?" Sully winced.

"Too many rocks," Stitch said. "Blech."

"It's not usually this quiet," Snow White finally finished. "Like it's waiting for something."

"It's a mountain." Hades tossed his ball of fire from hand to hand. "Trust me, kitten, they don't change much."

Snow White had never been this deep in the mine and had not realized that the mountain was quite this big. The tunnel went on and on, seemingly never changing.

"I thought you said there were gems?" Tiana asked.

Snow White felt her cheeks go hot. "There are! Or there usually are. It's not at all the way I remember it. There used to be separate tunnels, glowing lanterns, positively thousands of jewels twinkling. Now it just seems . . . well, quite dead."

"Please don't say the D-word when there's a million pounds of stone overhead," Rapunzel pled.

"Which D-word?" Hades counted on his fingers. "Defenestration? Demesne? Despot? Detritus? Diabolic? Dodecahedron?"

"D-e-a-t-h," Rapunzel whispered back through clenched teeth.

"Oh! Death! That's my middle name. I say it all the time."

"Then what's your last name?"

"Oh, it's also Death."

"Y'all need to—Wait. I think I see something." Tiana grabbed an empty lantern sitting on the ground and held it out to Hades, who flicked a finger at it to kindle a smaller blue fire within. Hurrying ahead, Tiana found a pickaxe leaning against a boulder. Just beyond it, the telltale sparkle of gems dotted the dark stone walls. "Finally!"

She set down the lantern and selected what appeared to be a huge diamond, using the pickaxe to pry it out.

"Ouch!"

Dropping the pickaxe, Tiana inspected her finger. "Of all the places to get a splinter, I swear. But wait . . ." She showed her finger to the group, and instead of a drop of blood, they saw a smear of a now-familiar acid green. "It's the Queen's poison! I need—"

But she didn't finish her sentence. Acid green seeped into her eyes, replacing the soft brown. Turning her back to her friends, she began to fiercely mine, grunting as she hacked into the stone again and again with a power and ferocity that Snow White found frightening.

"What's Tiana doing?" she asked.

"Whistling while she works," Hades replied.

Sulley stepped up. "I think I know what to do." He gently grasped Tiana around the waist and pulled her away from the wall, murmuring, "Come on, Tia. You're gonna hurt yourself, going at it like that."

But instead of laughing it off and thanking him for caring, Tiana struggled out of his grasp and whirled on him, holding up the pickaxe like she was facing off with a Fractured goon.

"I need these gemstones," Tiana growled.

Her job was to make potions to heal the others, and if she didn't have gemstones, she didn't have potions. Therefore, there was nothing more important than gemstones.

The sparkling, glorious gemstones singing their soft cloying song.

"Well, sure," Sulley responded reasonably, paws up. "But—"

Before he could finish, Tiana took a swipe at him with the poisoned pickaxe, and he danced back to avoid getting struck. When he was out of range, she turned back to the wall and began hacking at it with the blade, again and again. Gems tumbled down with the rocks and scree, but it didn't satisfy her. They weren't enough. She didn't even pick them up. There were more gems, better gems, still stuck in the wall. She had to get them out, had to gather as many as she could.

What if someone got hurt, and there was no healing potion? Why, without her potions, her team could die. They would suffer. They would hate her. She'd grown up knowing that hard work was the only way forward, that she couldn't rest, couldn't dance and sing, not when there was work to do. Her father had taught her the value of hard work, and if she let down her friends, it was like letting him down.

She couldn't have that.

She couldn't let them down.

She couldn't let Mickey down.

She couldn't let *anyone* down.

She would gather so many gemstones that she would never run out of potions. Her friends would never have to suffer. She would never have to look in anyone's eyes as they lay on the ground, begging and pleading for help, and tell them that if only she'd mined a few more gems, maybe she would have that lifesaving potion.

She would keep mining.

She would keep mining no matter what.

"I can't believe she almost hit me. That's definitely not Tiana," Sulley said. "She's like the Huntsman. She's been flooded with bad magic! What do we do?"

In response, footsteps marched along the track behind them, the sound of feet and boots on stone echoing down the tunnel. When Hades turned and held up the glowing blue flame in his palm, the shapes of four Fractured goons appeared, getting closer with every step.

———◇———

11

In that moment, Snow White realized that Tiana had been acting as the de facto leader, and now that she was ensorcelled and furiously mining, no one quite knew what to do. Snow White looked to Rapunzel and Sulley, and they were each in position to fight, weapons at the ready, but neither offered strategic plans. Stitch was a bit of an uncontrollable wild card, already glowing with fire as he prepared to battle, and Hades . . . well, he was too morally ambiguous to be in charge of anything and was merely rolling the ball of fire back and forth over his fingers like he was vaguely bored by the prospect of a fight.

"Does anyone know anything about healing?" Snow White asked.

"Just that Tiana, or the other healers—Captain Jack or Baymax—always handles it," Sulley answered. "Every team of Guardians usually gets one healer, and that healer isn't supposed to get really, really obsessed with mining."

Snow White considered the scene before her. The cave was barely as tall as Sulley and just wide enough for him, Rapunzel, and Stitch to stand side by side without touching. Hades hung back as usual, waiting to see if he was needed. If Snow White joined the goon fight, there wouldn't have been room for her to even swing her pickaxe.

"I'll see if Tiana has any more healing potions," she said.

"Let us know if you find any beignets!" Rapunzel said, right before launching herself forward with a mighty swing of her frying pan.

As the fight began, Snow White hurried to Tiana, who was completely oblivious to the goons, all her focus solely on the act of mining. She didn't even seem that interested in the gemstones she'd plucked from the wall as they'd mounded at her feet and were strewn around the cavern.

"I hope this is the right thing to do," Snow White said, reaching for Tiana's bag. "I do apologize for invading your personal space, but, well, it's a bit of an emergency. Hopefully you'll thank me later."

Fortunately, Tiana was so intent on her task that she didn't seem to care or even notice that Snow White was gently pawing through her bag. There really was some sort of magnificent magic about the small, crescent-shaped pouch: it was a lot bigger on the inside, with warm light shining on dozens of potions arranged on shelves that certainly couldn't exist inside a regular cloth bag. Snow White recognized the tubes of healing potions, but all the other concoctions were a mystery. Most of them looked dangerous, swirling blood red or inky indigo. As she sorted through them with her entire upper body inside the bag, impossible as it was, she finally saw what she needed—the potion Tiana had used to change the Huntsman and mutated squirrels back to normal.

But there was only one potion left.

"There you are!" she said, grabbing the bottle and reversing out of the bag and back into the cavern, which felt noticeably darker and more confining.

"Keep mining," a dull voice said, and she spun

around to find a Fractured goon standing right there, its axe already slicing toward her.

Even with her newfound abilities, the goon had surprised her, and Snow White couldn't dodge. The axe slammed into her shoulder, and the potion flew from her hand, clattering against the stone. The pauldrons of her rosewood armor helped, but she still felt the sting, and then that arm went numb.

Casting about for her pickaxe, she found it leaning against the cave wall where she'd left it, but the goon was already swinging up with its weapon, and she barely avoided getting clocked on the chin. Spinning to the side, she dodged the strike, then ducked under the next hit and grabbed her pickaxe while in a crouch. She managed to jab the Fractured goon in the gut, knocking it back, but there wasn't really room for her to fully swing her huge weapon and take advantage of its powerful arc.

"How's Tiana doing? Back to normal yet?" Rapunzel called.

"I found the potion, but I can't—" Snow White dropped to her knee and rolled to avoid the goon's next strike, then slashed down with her pickaxe, finally landing a hit. "It rolled away. There are more goons!"

"Hades, we need you!" Rapunzel shouted.

Hades looked up from where he dramatically lounged against the wall. "Nah, you all have this. You need the exercise."

"It's funny how you're lazy about everything except running your mouth," Sulley said. "Wait, no. That's not actually funny. It's annoying."

Hades sighed. "If I must. Hey, Snow—you ready to tag out?"

Snow White looked up. "Am I ready to what?"

An even bigger sigh. "Just get out of the way and get Tiana back to being busy in a useful way instead of an obnoxious way."

As he approached, smoke billowed off his robes and the flame in his hand grew brighter. His grin curled up, his eyes narrowing in a sinister fashion. "Maybe I'll enjoy this after all."

Snow White rolled away from the goon right as Hades surprised it with a fireball. It turned away from her to face the new challenge, and she exhaled in relief and crawled over to the potion she'd dropped. The glass had cracked, but the tube wasn't completely broken; half the potion was still inside, while the other half had leaked onto the stone and was irretrievable. As she watched Tiana, trying to figure out how to get close without triggering a defensive response, the battle raged on behind her. She heard one Fractured goon explode into crystals, but she also heard her friends grunting as they took damage. After this fight, they would need Tiana and her healing skills more than ever.

The problem, as she saw it, was that Tiana was focused on mining, her arms moving mechanically up and down as she drove the pickaxe into the wall. There was no way to get the bottle to her lips without breaking it further—or activating her rage. But there had to be something she could do. If only she had some food . . .

Snow White remembered her pickaxe growing from other tools, right when she needed it most. The wood always felt alive in her hands, the roses and leaves that entwined the weapon a living part of its power. Carefully setting the potion down so that it wouldn't leak more, she picked up her pickaxe and closed her eyes. Her fingers wrapped around the handle, and it was as if she could feel the energy vibrating through the wood, feel her connection to her beloved forest and all the animals and plants there.

"I need berries," she whispered to the pickaxe, and to the magic, and maybe to the powers deep within herself. "Edible berries. Please. My friend—all my friends—are in danger."

A thrum of warmth tingled up her fingertips, the scent of a hot summer day tickling her nose. She could picture raspberry bushes in the shade, their berries heavy and sweet as bees and birds landed here and there, feasting with a sleepy buzz. When she opened her eyes, a bright green raspberry vine wrapped around the blade of her pickaxe, fat red berries gleaming. She set down her pickaxe, plucked the berries, and poured a little potion on them.

"I hope this works," she murmured.

She picked up her pickaxe and edged toward Tiana, acting nonchalant and nonthreatening. Reaching from below, she slipped a berry into Tiana's open mouth. Without breaking her speed, without so much as blinking, Tiana mechanically chewed and swallowed. Snow White kept on feeding her potion-dipped berries, occasionally glancing at the fight beyond. The Guardians had taken down two more Fractured goons, leaving, as always, the biggest and most powerful one to defeat last.

It was like an elegant dance, the way they combined their skills. Rapunzel lashed out with her frying pan, then retreated as Sulley landed an uppercut with his door shield. Before the goon could recover, Stitch charged it, slamming into its belly like a ball of living fire, and as Stitch rolled away to safety, Hades hit the goon in the face with a thrown fireball. Snow White wasn't sure how she could ever fit into this choreography, but she knew she was doing her best. After the fight, the others would need Tiana's skills as a healer. Everyone had a unique part to play.

Her pickaxe helpfully kept making berries, but she was running out of potion, and she was painfully aware that it was the last one of its kind left in Tiana's bag.

"Come on," she whispered as she popped another berry in Tiana's mouth. "Come back to us."

Sweat had broken out over Tiana's face, and her lips were now stained with the potion she so desperately needed. Her arms trembled with the effort of mining so hard for so long. Snow White dipped a raspberry in the last bit of potion and guided it to Tiana's mouth. If this didn't work, she'd have to start dragging berries through the dirty potion on the floor, and the thought repulsed her.

With a crystalline crash, the final goon was gone, and the other Guardians gathered around Snow White and Tiana. As they watched, Tiana's pickaxe slammed into the wall . . . and stuck there. She released the wooden handle and stumbled back, looking at her hands.

"What happened?" she asked. "What happened to my hands?"

They all looked down, and her hands were indeed a mess of blisters, bruises, and cuts from the rough wood of the pickaxe, all tinted with the remaining smears of the green poison. She turned to face Snow White, her face a sweaty mask of confusion.

"The Queen's poison," Snow White explained. "It was on the pickaxe, and you got a splinter. There was barely enough potion to bring you back."

Tiana reached for her bag and looked inside, frowning. "We're gonna need some more of that magic soon. Seems like the Queen gets her claws into everything around here." She glanced around the mine, suddenly noticing that everyone else was looking the worse for wear. "What happened to y'all?"

"Goons," Hades said, obviously the least damaged from the fight. "Purple cracks, big weapons, yadda yadda. You know how it is."

Looking tired but determined, Tiana handed out glass vials of her healing potion, and everyone took one—except Snow White and Hades. "I only took one hit," Snow White said. "And it seems like we need to conserve potions for when we really need them."

Tiana pointed to the mound of gemstones at her feet. "Okay, but we need you in top form, so if anything hurts at all, it's better to take the potion and let me make more. I have plenty of ingredients now." She reached for a particularly large emerald and winced. "Maybe we can split a potion. The only thing that hurts more than my hands is my back. This mining gig is not for me. I'll take running my restaurant and fighting baddies any day."

She and Snow White each drank half a healing potion, and Snow White didn't realize just how hurt she had been until the pain went away. She was accustomed to helping anyone in any way she could, but it certainly took a toll on the body, fighting alongside the Guardians.

Once everyone was healed and ready and Tiana had scooped all the gemstones into her magically voluminous bag, Hades stepped forward.

"Which way are we going?" he asked. "Because don't get me wrong, I love being underground. It's kind of my thing. But this mine is definitely looking a bit . . . Fractured. And that is definitely *not* my thing."

He held his blue flame up to the stone wall, showing purple cracks growing out of the floor and up into the ceiling. Snow White was certain they hadn't been there before, but the goons had distracted her from looking too closely at the scenery.

"We came in here for the gems, and we have the gems," Tiana said. "So let's get out of here. Does the tunnel go out the other side of the mountain?"

"Why, I don't know." Snow White tried hard to think if Dopey, Doc, Bashful, Sleepy, Sneezy, Happy, or Grumpy had ever mentioned such a thing, but they didn't talk much of mining back home; they preferred to leave work at work. "I know they always go in and out through the same opening, so I suppose this tunnel and the tracks must eventually have a dead end. I'm surprised we haven't reached it yet."

"Whew, good, let's get out of here!" Rapunzel said, picking up the lantern Tiana had left behind when she began mining. "Because if I have to choose between sunshine and endless darkness, I'm always gonna choose sunshine. Plus, Pascal turns kinda gray without it."

She headed back the way they'd come, and Snow White's heart felt a little lighter as she followed. They had the gems they needed, and once they were back outside, she knew the way to the Queen's castle—hopefully.

The cave, however, had different ideas. The mountain began to rumble, making tiny rocks tumble down from the ceiling. As the trembling built, the entire cavern began to shake, and Snow White was thrown into the wall as she struggled to stay upright.

"Run!" Rapunzel shouted.

But the cave seemed to hear her, and with an echoing boom, the tunnel collapsed, blocking their way out with a wall of boulders threaded with glowing purple cracks.

They were trapped.

12

In the silence that followed the cave-in, Snow White struggled to breathe through the debris in the air. Her eyes were squeezed shut against the dust, her ears ringing with the enormous crash. As she blinked madly, she found the cave completely blocked without a single ray of light from outside.

"Okay, fine, I don't like caves anymore," Hades shouted, one finger in his ear. "Maybe I'll put some skylights in the Underworld when I get back home." The only light now came from his hair, Rapunzel's lantern, and the pulsating purple cracks that seemed to be growing with every passing moment.

"Um, okay, this is . . . this is a cave-in . . . another cave-in. . . . Everyone, this is not okay," Rapunzel said, breathing so fast that Snow White was concerned for her. Pascal peeked out of her hair, looking as concerned as a chameleon could look.

"We're going to be fine," Tiana said firmly. "We just go around using another path."

"I can't breathe!" Rapunzel yelped. "It's just like . . . this one time Eugene and I were in a cave-in, and the water was rising, and we were trapped, and it was so dark, and, and—I can't breathe!"

Snow White was closest, so she set down her pickaxe and reached over to take Rapunzel's hand in both of her own. "There's no water," she said in her calmest voice, the one she often used for hurt animals. "No water at all. The cave is dry, and only one side is blocked. See? The other way is wide open. We have light and air and there is no water and you're not alone. We're here with you."

"But I can't—" Rapunzel choked out a sob. "It's like it's happening all over again, even though it isn't. I can't stop shaking!"

"Then just shake," Snow White told her. "Why, just let it move right through you. Feelings are like the weather, you know—they change all the time. Your body knows what to do, and your mind will catch up. Take deep breaths and focus on the lantern light. Or Hades's hair, but the lantern is a bit warmer."

"Not as handsome, though," Hades added. "That lantern isn't debonair at all."

"Now, let's breathe in and out. In . . . and out." As Snow White led Rapunzel through some deep breaths, she felt eyes on her and looked up to see Tiana watching the interaction with intense curiosity. Snow White wasn't used to such scrutiny, so she blushed and turned back to Rapunzel, who was breathing more regularly.

"Do you think you can start moving now?" Snow White gently asked Rapunzel. "You might feel better if you move away from the rocks and toward fresh air."

"Fresh air sounds nice," Rapunzel said, her voice shaky. "Thanks for that, Snow. You really have a way with—"

"Calming frightened animals?" Hades broke in.

"Calming frightened *people*," Rapunzel corrected.

"So I guess we leave the other way," Tiana said.

She began walking, and Rapunzel held her hair up out of the rock dust and picked her way carefully through the rubble. Snow White followed her, and everyone else followed Snow White, who began to feel as if the mountain were pressing down on her, squeezing the air out of her lungs and the hope out of her heart. She could be calm to help Rapunzel, but deep inside, she shared her fear. The tunnel should've ended long ago. And yet here they were, trapped with nowhere else to go except down a tunnel that appeared endless.

Just ahead, Tiana gasped and threw out her arms, and Snow White barely stopped in time to avoid falling into a chasm. The ground just . . . ended. Maybe twenty feet away, the tunnel continued, but there was no bridge, no ledge, no way to traverse the open space.

"Well, that's inconvenient," Hades said.

Rapunzel stepped up to study it. "There has to be some way across."

"I have . . . idea." Stitch took a deep breath and began to grow, but Snow White put a hand on his arm.

"We don't know how deep it goes," she told him. "We can't risk letting you fall down there, if it's deeper than you are tall."

And, as Snow White thought but did not say, it probably wasn't the best time to stress Stitch out and have him get stuck in a different form again, in a cave that already lacked any room to maneuver.

"Wait!" They all looked at Rapunzel, who held her lantern up to show the other edge of the chasm. "See that . . . stala . . . thingy on the other side of the pit?"

Snow White saw several of them, lining the other side like teeth.

"Stalagmite," Hades supplied. "It has a *G* for *ground*, whereas stalactite has a *T* for *top*." When everyone looked at him in surprise, he shrugged. "What? I know things. Some things. Underground things, mostly."

"What about it?" Sulley asked Rapunzel.

Rapunzel gave her lantern to Tiana, hung her frying pan from her belt, and began to unwind her hair. "I'm going to loop my hair over it to make a bridge."

"Is that safe?" Tiana asked.

"Probably not, but we don't have a lot of options, and I really, really need to get out of here." Tying her hair into a lasso, Rapunzel twirled it in the air and slung it across the chasm. The first two tosses didn't work, but the third time, it landed neatly around a stalagmite, and she pulled it tight.

"Do we . . . walk across it?" Hades asked. "Because that's pretty weird. I mean, I can kind of float, but it's weird for everyone else."

"You can use it however you want," Rapunzel said. She laid a length of her hair down on the ground.

"Sulley, if you stand on this end, it'll anchor it for everyone else. And, uh, it'll pull on my scalp less."

Sulley put his foot down on Rapunzel's hair, muttering, "Sorry."

Tiana was the first one to walk across Rapunzel's hair like a tightrope, then Hades, who did kind of float. Stitch scampered across like a six-legged squirrel. Snow White was scared so she used her pickaxe to help her balance. She was very, very careful not to look down, and she thought distinctly happy thoughts all the way across. When it was just Sulley and Rapunzel left, Tiana unlooped Rapunzel's hair, and Rapunzel towed it back in.

"Uh-oh," she said. "I didn't think about this part."

"I did." Sulley picked her up and shouted, "Stitch, get big and catch her!" Before she could object, the big, furry monster tossed Rapunzel across the chasm. She yelped and flailed, and Stitch, now Sulley's size, easily caught her.

"But Sulley, how will you—" she began, trying to get her hair back into place.

Taking a running start, Sulley leapt across the chasm, barely catching the other ledge in one paw before hauling himself up and over.

"Wait, you could do that all along?" Rapunzel asked.

"Yeah, but nobody else could. And I didn't want to throw my shoulder out, pitching everybody across. The hair tightrope was a good move."

Now that they were safely across the crevasse, they kept walking, picking up the pace. Snow White wanted so badly to be out of the mountain, and she was fairly certain that if she ever found her way back outside, she'd never go underground again. She probably wouldn't even like cleaning under the bed.

Holding the lantern to light the way, Tiana strode confidently forward. "You know, this isn't—" she began.

Slam!

Crunch!

She stumbled back, the cavern gone dark.

The lantern was gone.

"What happened?" Rapunzel asked. "Where'd the light go?"

"Hades, come up here. But don't go past my hand." Tiana waited, and when Hades moved to the front of the group, the light from his fiery blue hair showed Tiana's outstretched hand.

"Okay, so is this a game of red light, green light or what?" he asked.

Tiana jabbed her hand forward and then back, quick as a whip.

Crunch!

This time, Snow White saw it—two boulders slammed in, one from either side of the cave. If Tiana hadn't moved her hand, it would've been pulverized, just like the crushed lantern at her feet.

"Okay, so now the Fractured cave has really aggressive doors," Hades muttered, stroking his chin. "How do we get past?"

"I'm going to wave my hand, and the moment the boulders are on their way back into place, jump through," she told him.

"Me first? Why me?"

"Because you're the god of death. If it doesn't work, you probably won't die."

"But it'll hurt. I hate hurting!"

"Tough. I can heal you. On the count of three, Blue Boy. One, two . . . three!"

Tiana's hand slashed forward, the boulders slammed together, and in the split second after that echoing smack, Hades bolted past them to the other side.

"Hey, I'm not dead, and it didn't hurt!" he said. "Your mileage may vary."

Rapunzel stepped up next and leapt through easily, although the boulders did slam on a few hairs, crimping them. Stitch catapulted through after her. And then only Tiana, Snow White, and Sulley were left.

"You got this?" Sulley asked Snow White.

"Everything we have to do scares me," she admitted. "But I keep getting through, so I just keep going."

"Yeah, that's how life works." He took a deep breath. "Hope I'm still as fast as I was in college."

Tiana counted to three, and Sulley bolted past the boulders. He screeched in pain and collapsed on the ground.

"My tail!" he howled. "It got pinched!"

"Snow, you ready?" Tiana said. "I'd better heal him before he brings the whole ceiling down with that caterwaulin'."

Snow White nodded, fidgeting with her pickaxe. She had never considered herself fast, but now she would find out if her new abilities included bypassing murderous boulders in evil caves. Her whole body was fizzing with nerves. When she fought the Fractured, it's like she had these confident instincts that sent signals to her limbs, like her body moved of its own volition, dangerous and with elegant precision. But there were apparently no such instincts for sprinting past boulders. She was in full control, and she couldn't mess up.

Even the tiniest mistake, just tripping on a pebble, might mean injuries too dire for Tiana's potions.

"I'm ready," she told Tiana, even though she didn't feel ready and probably never would.

"One, two, three!"

Slam went the boulders, and then Snow White ran with everything she had. She felt the air swoosh by as the boulders closed again, but she'd made it past, and she hadn't gotten anything squashed at all. She gave a big sigh and leaned against the cold stone wall. Stitch silently took her hand with two of his and squeezed reassuringly.

Tiana didn't have to count for herself; she just flashed her hand and then did a diving roll between the receding boulders. Once they were all safely beyond the trap, she gave Sulley her second-to-last healing potion for his crunched tail, and finally the cave went quiet again.

"You're in front now, Blue Boy," she told Hades. "Until we find another lantern, you're our only source of light."

"Oh, goodie," he grumbled. "I'm literally the canary

in the coal mine. Or the blue jay in the diamond mine. Either way, I refuse to sing. Unless there's karaoke."

Still, he moved to the front and even seemed to glow brighter, as if actually trying to be useful without being asked for once. The tunnel went on and on, and everyone was jumpy, waiting for the next peril to appear. At least the ceiling opened up a bit so it wasn't so cramped. Snow White was glad to be in the middle of the group, neither first nor last. The mine wasn't a place where she felt competent, even with her newfound powers.

"Ugh!" Hades said from up front. "Why is the ground sticky? Did someone spill something?"

"We're the only people in the evil mine," Tiana reminded him. "And we just got here, so it must be something else."

"Slime?" Sulley offered. "I know a few slime monsters."

Something hissed overhead, and Snow White clutched her pickaxe and watched with growing horror as a huge form slowly emerged from the darkness overhead. Dangling by a single purple thread, a spider bigger than Sulley descended and landed on eight hairy legs, glowing with those familiar violet cracks.

Eight white eyes shone brightly as it opened its gigantic fanged mouth to hiss again.

"This is my first Fractured spider," Hades admitted "Does anyone have a really, really big rolled-up newspaper?"

But Rapunzel already had her frying pan out and at the ready and wasn't waiting for permission to start the fight. "I don't know what a newspaper is," she said, smacking the spider with a spinning slash, "but I've got a frying pan."

The spider's eight white eyes seemed to narrow with insult as it shook its head and struck at Rapunzel, its fangs dripping purple venom.

"I don't think he likes you," Hades noted.

"Stop quipping and fight!" Rapunzel shouted.

With more room in the cave, the Guardians and Snow White spread out around the spider and took turns hitting it while dodging its fangs. It seemed to take more hits than the regular goons, and their attacks were more difficult thanks to the bits of sticky web on the floors and stretching out from the walls. Snow White got a boot caught in a strand and had to slice the web off with her pickaxe.

"Take that!" Hades shouted, slamming the spider with fire.

"And that!" Rapunzel added, smacking it with her frying pan.

"And also this!" Snow White said, whirling her pickaxe around for a solid strike to the furry purple abdomen.

To her astonishment, the giant cave spider exploded into purple shards, its webs disappearing along with it. Snow White looked at her pickaxe in awe. She hadn't done it alone, but still, she couldn't believe that she'd contributed the final strike.

"Nice job, new kid," Hades said.

"Oh, thank you!" Snow White couldn't stop smiling.

Even better, once the spider was no longer blocking the tunnel, they could see a bright glow somewhere up ahead.

"Sunlight!" Rapunzel called.

She broke out in a run, and everyone followed.

"Stop, we need to go slowly! There could be more traps!" Tiana shouted, but desperation won out over caution. As they charged down the tunnel, weapons ready, expecting the next trap at any time, the square of light grew bigger and bigger and bigger. Finally, they burst out into the daylight, and Snow White inhaled a deep breath of air as she squinted, waiting for her eyes to adjust.

"Where are we?" Rapunzel asked.

"Somewhere really annoyingly, stupidly bright," Hades said.

Once Snow White could see again, her heart fell.

"I don't know where we are," she told the others. "This place is completely unfamiliar. But I don't think we're anywhere near the Queen's castle. And I don't know how to find it."

———◇———

13

Snow White had hoped that they would emerge from the mine entrance as if they'd never even made the journey down that long dark harrowing tunnel; she figured that a Fractured cave might force them into danger and then spit them right back out where they began. But instead, they were on the side of an unfamiliar mountain, surrounded by tall trees and heavy scrub. There was no waterfall, no river, no log to cross; just a rough deer trail zigzagging down and around the mountain, which was indeed much bigger than it seemed.

"Maybe this trail leads all the way around the outside, to the other side of the mountain, the part I know," Snow White said. "If I can just find something familiar, we can set our course for the Queen's castle."

"So you've never been here before?" Hades asked.

Snow White shook her head. "I don't think so. Everything's changed so much that it's hard to tell."

"So you've never seen that beautiful glowing castle surrounded by clouds before? That's not, you know, the place we're trying to reach? I mean, how many castles does one world need, honestly?"

Hades was a little ahead on the trail, and Snow White hurried to see what he was pointing at. It wasn't the Queen's castle—Snow White knew that place quite well, and a dark and dangerous place it was indeed—but this new palace certainly was beautiful in its own right.

"Why, I've never seen that castle before in my life!" she said, stunned. "The Queen's castle isn't like that at all. It's practically repulsive. But . . . well, one day I met a handsome prince. I always wondered where he'd come from, but I couldn't exactly go looking for a prince on my own in my scullery clothes, could I? Not with the Queen's huntsman stalking the forest. This castle looks like exactly the kind of place we might find the mysterious prince. Perhaps he can help us get our bearings."

Tiana elbowed her in the ribs. "You wanna go see the handsome prince, huh? No complaints here."

Annoyingly, Snow White couldn't stop herself from blushing. "I think we need any help we can get right now. Maybe he can take us to the Queen's castle and help us save my friends."

"Mm-hmm." Rapunzel elbowed her from the other side. "We definitely need to go check out that castle. *For strategic reasons.*"

Snow White was flustered as she led them down the trail and around the mountain, keeping her eyes pinned to the glowing castle on the horizon. It almost looked like it was nestled among the clouds, and she couldn't help daydreaming about the handsome prince. She'd always longed to see him again, and even if her world was in danger, she wouldn't mind running into him. Perhaps he would be willing to help fight the Fractured Magic infecting their land. Perhaps they could fight it together.

Although . . . this part of the world didn't seem quite as Fractured as the mine and the dark forest. These trees stood tall and strong, the animals were friendly and curious, and there were no telltale purple cracks suggesting that more goons might be around every corner. The sun shone down, and soon they discovered a well-kept road. The closer they got, the more glorious the castle appeared, as if it were a lovingly handmade toy placed among fluffy spun sugar, and by late afternoon, Snow White could count the windows and see the crest on every pennant. The castle was real, and they had almost reached their goal.

One thing was bothering her, though.

She wasn't seeing any of the usual traffic she would have expected around a thriving castle. No wagons going in and out, no guards marching around the wall. The castle was utterly still, aside from the pennants waving in the wind. Still, there were no purple cracks, no goons, no reasons to think anything might be wrong. She didn't speak her worries aloud; perhaps she was just being paranoid.

As they trod the path up to the portcullis, Tiana looked around, similarly suspicious. "Anybody else think there's something peculiar about this place?"

"Just the fact that I don't have a castle this nice," Hades complained. "What's the point of being a god if somebody has a better castle than you?"

"There's no one here," Snow White said, ignoring Hades.

"Right? I know castles, and castles are full of people," Rapunzel added. "Good castles, at least. Lone towers in the middle of nowhere chosen specifically for their solitude, not so much."

As they entered the gatehouse, everyone had their weapon at the ready. Snow White's fingers were white where they clutched her pickaxe; she expected some kind of attack at any moment. Sulley moved in front as they neared the main entrance, and Stitch began to heat up, just in case.

"Let's not be hasty," Snow White said nervously. "We don't want to appear too dangerous. Maybe there's a reason for the quietude."

Sulley stepped inside the castle proper like he was expecting an ambush, but none came. It was beautiful within, glowing white marble threaded with pink and gold that magnified the afternoon sun's resplendence. Velvet curtains swagged around stained glass windows, their bejeweled tassels sweeping the floor as they perfectly framed beautiful scenes that shimmered with sunbeams. Snow White pointed to one of the grand stained glass windows, a rainbow-hued portrait of someone very familiar.

"That's him! That's the Prince!" she squealed.

"My lady?"

She looked to the dais and saw—

"My lord?"

It was him, the Prince, the one she'd met by the well so long ago and longed to meet again. He looked exactly as she remembered him, handsome and strong and kind. His crimson cape swirled behind him as he hurried across the throne room, his eyes alight and his lips set in a brilliant smile.

"I returned to the well so many times, my lady, but I never found you. That castle—it's become corrupted, treacherous. I was so worried for you," he began.

"Oh, yes, I—I never go there anymore. Except for now. There's a problem, you see. . . ."

She trailed off, looking into his sky-blue eyes. Her heart swelled, her stomach fizzing with butterflies. She held her pickaxe in one hand, and the Prince took her other hand between his own. A jolt of electricity went up her arm, making her blush.

"A problem? Then how can I help?" he asked.

"It's my stepmother, the Queen," she told him, lost in his eyes. "She's kidnapped my friends and is using a magic mirror to spread the darkness in our land."

"Then my soldiers and I will face her," he said. "We'll help however we can." He stepped closer. "Whatever you require."

She looked around the empty, echoing hall. "But where are your soldiers? Where is everyone?"

He laughed it off. "Oh, they're preparing for tonight's ball."

"A ball?"

"Of course. Our people have been so concerned with the evil sweeping the land that we thought holding a ball might distract them, cheer them up. But now that you're here—you and your friends—I must insist we throw the ball in your honor so that we can join together in goodwill before taking this fight to the Queen. You'll come, won't you? Please say you will."

Snow White blushed and looked down at her outfit. "That's ever so kind, and I do love a ball, but . . . well, we've been traveling, and I'm afraid we don't have anything proper to wear to a formal affair."

"Why can't we wear what we have on?" Rapunzel asked. "I think we all look pretty great!"

"I never wear shoes," Sulley said, shuffling his big, hairy feet. "I hope that's not a problem, Your Majesty."

"Of course not." The Prince smiled at them all, his arms spread wide as if to embrace them. "I'm sure we can accommodate all your needs. My lady, I am pleased to meet your friends, but might I ask: are they from a realm beyond our own? For I have never seen such curious beings."

Snow White looked to Tiana for an answer, but Tiana raised her eyebrows and nodded back, urging Snow White to keep talking.

"They are indeed from different . . . realms. They are pledged to fight the Fractured Magic—the dark magic that has spread throughout the land—and they were sent here to help us banish it from our land. Why, I can only imagine the worlds they describe, and I do hope to see them one day." Much to her embarrassment, she broke off in a yawn. Breakfast seemed ever so far away, and their sleep had been much disturbed.

The Prince bowed. "You must be tired. If you'd like, I can have the staff show you to the baths, and perhaps we can find suitable attire while you relax and wait for the banquet?"

"You had me at 'baths,' " Tiana said, blowing a wayward curl out of her eyes.

"Banquet," Sulley and Stitch said at the same time with equal reverence.

But Hades stepped forward, eyes narrowed. "Okay, fine, so I'll talk about the blue elephant in the room. If you think those of us who aren't human look weird, are your guests going to react poorly? You know—running, shouting, pitchforks and torches, that sort of thing? Because it honestly gives me indigestion."

"You will be treated with the utmost respect," the Prince assured him. "In our land, we sometimes encounter magical creatures and people, but we judge those we meet by their hearts, not their forms. Once our citizens know you're on our side and fighting against the spread of the dark magic—and I'll be sure they know—you'll be honored as heroes."

Hades nodded and stepped back. "Then I'm in."

"Everything does sound delightful." Snow White looked deep into the Prince's guileless blue eyes. "If it's not too much trouble."

"You could never be trouble," he said, taking her hand and bowing to kiss it. He stood and clapped, and servants ran in from multiple doors, all neatly dressed in matching livery and smiling politely. "Please take our guests downstairs to relax in the baths. They'll require proper raiment for tonight's ball. Treat them all with dignity and respect, for they are our guests of honor!"

A trio of servants beckoned Snow White, Tiana, and Rapunzel in one direction, while a stuffy-looking valet blinked in surprise at Hades, Sulley, and Stitch before clearing his throat and herding them in the other direction. The valet had clearly seen his share of strange people, or perhaps he was just too well trained to allow more than a moment of shock to cross his haughty features.

"Oh, great," Hades moaned. "Just me and the other blue monsters being herded away underground. How fitting. How not at all like the Underworld. I feel very special, as befits a god."

"I didn't know gods complained so much," Tiana whispered to the young women, which got them giggling loud enough to drown out whatever else Hades found displeasing.

Following the staff, Snow White and the women ascended a twisting staircase and followed a long stone hall decorated with sumptuous carpets and colorful tapestries. They were led to a room lined in perfectly painted tiles and lit with colorful hanging lamps, but the most arresting items in the room were four huge copper bathtubs, already filled with perfumed water and clouding the space with steam.

"First!" Rapunzel cried, already struggling with the ties on her dress.

"There's plenty to go around," Tiana mused. "But, still: second."

The servants bowed out and closed the door, leaving the trio to undress behind screens and slip into the rose-scented tubs. Even if she was a princess, Snow White had never really felt like one, not since the evil queen had come into her life. She'd never enjoyed such a luxurious bath, the water hot and full of bubbles and rose petals. She relaxed down into the water, feeling the dirt of the road and the dust of the fights drain away. When the servants returned, she let one wash her hair, noting with disgust the filth that sloughed off with each pitcher of warm water.

"This is the life," Tiana murmured.

Rapunzel held up a rubber ducky as three of the servants rubbed suds through her hair, which took up the entire extra bathtub. "So much better than a creek."

Once the baths had gone cold, the young women were wrapped in fluffy robes and given soft slippers. The servants sat them down while they dried and coiffed their hair. Soon the servants led them to another room, where armoires were stuffed full of ball gowns.

"Can we go back to the baths?" Rapunzel asked, but Tiana hip-bumped her.

"Let's get our girl ready to dance with the Prince, huh?"

At that, Rapunzel brightened. "Yes! Primping for a purpose! I'm in."

Sorting through the dresses, Snow White gravitated toward a confection in shades of blue that matched the

Prince's eyes. It fit like a glove, almost like it had been made just for her. She clapped for Tiana's sleeveless dress in shades of green and champagne and helped Rapunzel select a mauve-and-lavender that wasn't too frilly.

"And look!" Rapunzel squealed. "It has pockets!"

Snow White missed the practical fit of her rose-wood armor and breeches, but she had to admit that she enjoyed the unusual sensation of being clean and feeling fancy, which had long been denied her by her stepmother.

"Ladies, it is almost time," a maid said nervously. She offered each of them a half mask embellished with glitter and jewels.

"Oh, so it's that kind of party," Tiana said, tying her flower-themed mask on with long satin ribbons.

"As long as it doesn't cover my mouth." Rapunzel took hers and made sure she could stick out her tongue. "I've got a lot of eating to do."

Snow White had never been to a masquerade ball before, although she'd heard of them. She tied on her mask, admiring the red roses adorning it. After being in so many fights recently, she worried that it limited her vision.

She picked up her pickaxe. "I've grown so accustomed to carrying it with me everywhere, but it doesn't quite go with the dress, does it?"

"Pickaxes and ball gowns don't match," Tiana agreed. "Not that we're expecting a fight, but I guess I can carry my smallest potion bag. And Rapunzel . . . well, there's no room for a frying pan on there."

"It would hit me in the hip while I danced," Rapunzel admitted. "I have space for Pascal, though, and that's what's important. And maybe I can slip something small into one of my pockets?"

Tiana plucked a hairpin from the dressing table and carefully slid it into Rapunzel's hair. "There. If anybody gives you trouble, jab 'em. Snow, you just focus on your prince. No purple cracks, hopefully no attacks."

As the staff led the trio back upstairs, Rapunzel turned to Snow White. "So how well do you know this guy again?" she whispered, quietly enough that the servants didn't hear.

Snow White thought back to their meeting at the well. "I don't know him well at all, and yet . . . I trust him. We have a real connection. Plus, he's a prince! And his servants certainly seem to love him. How could he be anything less than perfect?"

"A lot of ways," Tiana muttered. "But . . . well, we're Guardians. If push comes to shove, we can always find a way to fight."

"There won't be any fighting!" Snow White said with a laugh. "It's a ball!"

But Tiana and Rapunzel exchanged a glance behind her back.

When the Fractured Mirror was around, no one was safe.

14

———◇———

Snow White, Tiana, and Rapunzel stood behind
a burgundy curtain. On the other side, the ball was
just starting, the attendees murmuring excitedly with
anticipation as they waited for the guests of honor to
arrive. The costumed herald turned to Tiana. "Your
name, miss?"

"Princess Tiana of Maldonia."

When he called, "Presenting Princess Tiana of
Maldonia!" she put on a regal smile and walked through
the curtain. Then it was Rapunzel's turn.

"Princess Rapunzel of Corona."

"Presenting Princess Rapunzel of Corona!"

Rapunzel grinned, murmured, "Here we go, Pascal. Time to smile and wave," and burst through the curtains.

Snow White realized in that moment that she had had no idea that the Guardians were princesses at all. What an odd coincidence, that she should meet two more princesses on this journey!

Then the herald turned to her. "Oh, just Princess Snow White, I suppose," she said nervously.

"Presenting Princess Snow White of I Suppose!" the herald called, and even though she was mortified, she put on her sweetest smile and swept into the ballroom.

Hundreds of masked people, most of them strangers, watched her with bright eyes and whispering lips. They clapped as she stepped down the red-carpeted stairs to join Tiana and Rapunzel.

"Er, King Hades, god of the Underworld, the Unseen, the Giver of Wealth, the Taker of Souls, the Renowned, Lord of the Abyss, greatest son of Cronus," the herald called, only slightly flustered.

Hades entered, waving magnanimously and wearing a mask made of smoke. "Can you believe they tried to make me take a bath?" he said when he reached them. "And the water wasn't even on fire!"

"Experiment 626 of the United Galactic Federation!" the herald called, and Stitch wandered down the steps, sniffing the air, in a formal suit with a cape. He had somehow managed to hide two of his arms, his antennae, and the spines on his back, making him look like a friendly and harmless dog dressed for a party. He waved to his friends and headed straight for the buffet. He wasn't wearing a mask, and Snow White realized she pitied the servant who'd been assigned to try to convince him to do so.

"James P. Sullivan, top Scarer of Monstropolis," the herald shouted, and Sulley nearly tore down the curtains as he tried to shuffle through a space that was clearly too small for him. He looked different without his armor—smaller. The fur on his head was slicked back in a pompadour, and like Stitch, he, too, wore a dramatic cape. This kingdom was apparently big on capes.

"Ladies and gentlefolk, our host: the Prince!"

The guests had politely clapped for every name called thus far, but they went simply mad when the Prince was announced. He entered through a different, grander door, and his cape was the most magnificent cape of all. Snow White felt like she was glowing inside as she watched him make his grand entrance. He was so handsome and confident, and the guests—his people— adored him. His feathered mask made his blue eyes sparkle—or maybe that was just the way he was looking at Snow White as he made a beeline directly for her.

"My lady, might I have the first dance?" he asked.

"Oh, yes! I'd be delighted!"

As if on cue, an orchestra on the balcony began to play a waltz, and he took her hand and spun her out onto the floor as the other guests backed up to give them a wide circle.

"You're a marvelous dancer," she told him.

"Then I'm glad my mother forced me to stay indoors and take all those lessons," he confided. "I hated it when I was younger, but now it's all worth it, if you'll keep dancing with me."

Other guests joined them as the Prince dipped and spun Snow White around and around until she was dizzy—or maybe that was something else making her so giddy. The Prince was an absolute gentleman, making polite conversation and showering her with compli- ments. He never stopped smiling at her, his eyes alight with fondness every time they met hers. The waltz concluded, and he led her to a punch bowl and offered her a crystal cup of something delightfully fizzy. As she sipped, she scanned the room for her friends and was happy to find them all pleasantly engaged.

Rapunzel had found the strawberries and was stuffing her mouth as Pascal sat on her shoulder eating a berry of his own, his scales a matching rosy pink. Tiana had found the cook and was happily arguing about the best flour for a proper rise on biscuits. Stitch was facedown in a tureen of soup while a kitchen cook begged him to return her ladle; he would likely never trust a ladle again, after what had happened at the cottage. Sulley had discovered a bored child and was busy making silly faces to make her smile. And Hades—well, maybe *pleasantly engaged* wasn't the correct term. He'd been cornered by an old woman who had a thousand questions about the afterlife and was grilling him on her future accommodations. Maybe he wasn't pleased, but at least he was occupied.

The Prince escorted Snow White to the buffet table, where she tasted delicacies she hadn't known since her early childhood, those happy, dreamlike days when both of her parents had been present and doting and she'd been treated as a real princess and not a scullery maid. She nibbled tea cakes and exotic fruits, supped on fine soups, and chomped on an array of cheeses. All the while, her conversation with the Prince carried on so easily, so naturally, that it was as if they'd known one another all their lives.

"My prince, a word?" a snooty steward said, nose in the air. "There's a problem with the evening's entertainment."

"Forgive me, my lady," the Prince said with a bow. "We have acrobats and actors waiting in the wings, and I need to make sure they have everything they need. Will you wait here for me?"

"Of course," Snow White said with a curtsy. "I don't mind keeping an eye on the buffet on your behalf while you're gone. Although I'll have to apologize in advance for whatever Stitch did with that ladle."

The Prince and the steward hurried off and disappeared behind a tapestry, and Snow White continued to sample the kingdom's sweets. Although she couldn't forget the reason she and the Guardians were there, and she was trying to find the right moment to ask the Prince how he and his soldiers planned to help fight the evil queen and her Fractured goons, she had to admit that this castle was a lovely place to be. Whoever married the charming Prince would be lucky to live in a place surrounded by such beauty, luxury, and peace.

"All good?" Tiana asked, appearing at her side.

"Oh, yes. He's exactly how I thought he'd be."

"Perfect?"

Snow White blushed. "Thoughtful and articulate and generous and a graceful dancing partner and—"

Tiana smirked. "Like I said, perfect."

"My lady." A servant had appeared at Snow White's side. "The Prince would like to speak with you on the balcony. Would you care to follow me?"

Snow White and Tiana shared an excited glance. "Yes, of course," Snow White said, and the servant bowed and led her toward a curtain pulled back to show moonlight on stone. She ducked past the heavy velvet and found herself alone on a glorious balcony overlooking a stunning garden. The scent of roses and gardenias washed over her with the starlit breeze as nightingales practiced their little trills in the blossom-laden boughs. Water splashed prettily in a fountain below, and the stone made secret paths through careful plantings of foamy wisteria. It was the most romantic thing she'd ever seen in her entire life, and that was before the Prince appeared, holding a single perfect red rose.

"Forgive me for leaving you alone," he said, head

bowed as he presented the flower. "My first loyalty is always to the kingdom."

"It should be no other way, Your Highness." She accepted the flower, and when he offered her his arm, she took that, too.

"Please, let's not be so formal. You needn't call me 'my lord' or 'Your Highness.' It would be nice to know at least one person with whom I could drop all the stuffy decorum. I'm not always stuffy, you know."

"Why, I don't think you're stuffy at all," she said sweetly, "but I'm happy to let no formalities stand between us. With me, you can just be exactly yourself, and that will always be enough."

"Your lips make music of every word, my lady."

Arms intertwined, they strolled along the railing of the balcony, which looked down into a peerless flower garden. Someone clearly cared for greenery and took great pains to coax bright blooms from every stem. How she longed to walk among the blowsy peonies and under arches of twining jasmine, hearing the sleepy thrum of bees on a summer afternoon!

"Would you like a closer look at the garden?" the Prince asked by her side, having noted her interest. "It shows better in the daytime, but night has its own secret beauty, does it not?"

"Oh yes, please," she said. "I always feel most at home among plants and animals and growing things."

The Prince steered her toward a stone staircase that spiraled regally down to the ground, with lanterns set at regular intervals to light the way. The moment Snow White's slippered feet touched the grass, it was as if she could sense the love in the garden, feel the touch of cool water and rich soil, the kiss of butterflies and the slow turning of worms underground. A doe and twin fawns emerged from a vegetable patch, greens hanging from their gentle mouths, and a family of rabbits looked up from their grazing to blink with wonder and welcome at their new guest.

"The garden seems to know you, my lady," the Prince murmured.

"Oh, do please call me Snow White. I'm not stuffy, either."

"Snow White," he said softly, gloved fingers stroking the creamy skin of her arm. "And your lips are rose red, your eyes the soft brown of a fawn treading in dappled sunlight." His shoulder bumped into hers, and she wanted to roll this moment up in her memory and think of it once a minute for the rest of her life. "You know, that day I met you by the well, I felt as if all my dreams were coming true."

"Yes, I . . . I know that feeling myself," she admitted.

"And then you disappeared, and I looked everywhere. I've sent my knights out into the forests to find you, but they've always returned with nothing to show. You're a mystery, sweet Snow White, and I did often wonder if I just imagined you."

A soft buzz caught Snow White's attention; a fat, fuzzy bee was bumbling a little too close. She moved her head away and laughed lightly. She had made a perfume of roses back at the cottage, and bees often momentarily mistook her for a flower.

"Oh, no, I'm very real, I assure you," she said. "But I've kept hidden, you see, for my stepmother, the Queen, wishes me harm. That's one of the reasons we're here. I mean, I didn't know if this castle was yours, but I hoped, and I'm so grateful that my hope was rewarded. But we're on our way to fight the Queen, for she has found a wicked weapon that's harming the land. Have the forests nearby become Fractured, with violet cracks and odd turnings in the paths?"

The bee bumped against her hair, its buzzing a little louder, and she—well, not swatted; she would never swat a bee, but she gently guided it away, toward the roses lining either side of the stone walkway.

"The cracks haven't yet reached us," he said, kneeling

to pluck another bright red rose. "But my knights have seen them elsewhere. We hear reports, and certainly strange things have been happening. The people are concerned."

"It will infect your kingdom, too, I'm afraid, unless we put a stop to it. Tomorrow we'll be on the road again, on our way to the Queen's castle, to try to stop it. The Queen has stolen my friends, and we must rescue them. Do you think . . . do you think you might be able to help?"

Instead of answering, the Prince hissed as if in pain and shook his hand.

"Have you been stung, your highness? I did see a bee, a confused little thing—"

But the Prince said nothing, not about helping her and not about the bee. He stood, and she waited for him to turn and present the newest rose to her and take both her hands in his and promise that he would help her fix this wrong, that he would stand up to evil for the good of his kingdom. But he just stared off into the forest, silent and still.

The rose fell from his fingertips and landed on the ground.

"I'm afraid I cannot," he said, and her hopes fell like shattered glass.

"But—but why? The evil will spread. If it's not yet at your doorstep, it soon will be!"

And finally the Prince turned to her, but he didn't take her hands. He reached for the ties of his mask and it fell away from his face, and when she saw his eyes fully revealed, she gasped.

Before, they'd been the deep blue of a summer sky, but now they were glowing a bright, poisonous green.

———⟡———

15

Snow White startled away from him and stumbled back.

The Prince had been poisoned.

"You—you—the Queen got to you!" she cried.

He smiled, and not his doting, adoring smile, but a sick and twisted leer. "Oh yes, you simpering fool, she got to me. One sting from her barb-tipped bee and I can finally see through your lies. Your silly adventure stops here. You cannot defeat the Queen and her minions. You're a weak, pathetic little scullery maid, a pretty face and nothing more. And this is as close as you will get to saving your friends. Your childish quest has failed."

The Prince whistled piercingly, and the sound of marching footsteps crunched within the forest. But were they his soldiers, or had the Queen sent more Fractured?

Snow White reached for her pickaxe, but of course it wasn't there. She'd left it in the castle, thinking no one could ever need a weapon at a ball.

What a fool she'd been.

"Tiana! Rapunzel! Guardians, help!" she screamed, but even as the words shredded her throat she knew no one would hear her. The loud orchestra, the babble of voices—no one was alert for cries for help from the garden down below.

"They can't save you now," the Prince said, hunching over like a stalking monster. "No weapon. No stronger protectors. No friends. You're all alone, and you're as helpless as a teeny, tiny mouse."

Snow White backed up, her mind hunting for some plan. . . .

He'd called her a mouse. And in her experience, even the smallest creatures could help, in some way.

"Birds! Mice! Creatures of the forest! Flowers and vines and roots! I need your help!" she called.

When she'd shouted for the Guardians, she'd felt uncertain and helpless, but as she called upon the forest, confidence swelled in her heart. It was as if her voice were amplified, her soul sending out a signal like a ringing bell.

And the forest responded in kind. Stags bounded out from the underbrush, brandishing their antlers. Snakes slithered from the shadows. Raccoons and badgers and rabbits rambled out onto the green, baring teeth that glinted in the moonlight. Owls flew to the nearest branches and clicked their beaks, *snip-snap*. Even bees and hornets awakened from their slumber and hung in the air, threatening with a grating buzz.

"Secure the Prince!" she shouted. "Carefully—he's ensorcelled!"

Vines of fragrant jasmine unwound from the nearby trellis and shot toward the Prince, ensnaring his wrists. Twisted roots speared out of the ground, their pointed tips wrapping around his ankles, shedding black dirt on his fine trousers. Thorn-tipped roses pinned his cape to the ground. He struggled and fought, and the stags surrounded him, the tines of their antlers holding him like a cage.

At the edge of the forest, six Fractured goons appeared, marching toward her in a row, their feet heedless of the careful plantings, crushing petals underfoot. Snow White had to move fast; she would soon be overrun.

"Nightingales! Go fetch the Guardians, please!" she called to the birds, and they rose up from the treetops in a mighty flock that whirled like a tornado before careening toward the open windows of the ballroom.

"Your little birdies and beasties can't stop the Queen," the Prince taunted. "They can't fight the Fractured. They'll be broken, ground to dust—"

With a slash of her hand, Snow White directed a jasmine vine over his mouth, silencing him.

"I know you don't mean any of that," she said, just in case the Prince—the real, good, true Prince—was aware of what was happening. "Sorry about this."

Smack!

Something struck her in the shoulder, hard enough to send her sprawling in the grass in her voluminous dress. She recognized that hot punch—an arrow shot by a Fractured goon.

They were closing in, weapons up.

Snow White stood and yanked out the arrow. Her fingers ached for her pickaxe, for any kind of weapon that would allow her to hit back and keep the villains at bay. She needed something big and hard and sharp, some way to fight back with power—

Wait.

She stumbled out of range behind a fountain and closed her eyes, reaching into the forest, searching for—

There.

"Come to me, if you will," she called, more with her heart than with her mind, and when she felt an answering thrum, she turned her attention back to the goons. She had to distract them until help arrived, keep them from attacking her en masse. Sensing her need, the owls took flight and swooped at the goons, slashing at them with razor-sharp talons, holding them off for a few more precious moments.

Right on time, answering her desperate call, a sleepy bear ambled out of the forest and stood on his hind legs, towering over the nearest goon. With a roar of annoyance, he swiped the goon with a mighty paw, and Snow White sent out a silent thanks to him for pausing his nap to offer his help.

But even if the bear was a mighty fighter, there were still too many goons, and they weren't just going to politely wait for the Guardians to arrive. Snow White's pickaxe was out of range, but, well, what was a pickaxe but wood and metal? And wood was one thing she had aplenty.

She ran to the nearest tree and put a hand to its ancient trunk, silently pleading for help, and a perfectly sized branch fell from the canopy. Its curve mimicked the blade of her pickaxe, and living leaves sprouted from it, its sap promising strength and sturdiness. When the next goon attacked, she leapt and sent her new stave carving through the air. The hit landed, solid and true, and Snow White grinned as she realized that she wasn't as hopeless and helpless as she'd once felt.

As she faced off with the goon, the animals and plants fought their own battles. Roots rose up and rocks rolled in, creating an obstacle course for her stumbling foes. Badgers bit them, raccoons used their clever little hands to pull vines taut as trip wires, hornets stung them relentlessly. Maybe the goons weren't people with thoughts and feelings who experienced pain, but they couldn't focus on attacking Snow White if they were completely covered in screeching, clinging squirrels.

Filled with a new confidence and satisfaction, she

doubled down on her attack, slashing and jabbing the nearest goon relentlessly with her living stave, giving the thoughtless monster no chance to recover or hit back. When it exploded into purple crystals, she wanted to stop and cheer for herself. Not only had she faced the goon alone and without real weapons, but she'd done so in a huge ball gown and dancing slippers.

As she turned to the next goon, she heard a bizarre sound, a shriek getting louder and louder. She turned to see Stitch running full force, big and burning with flame, his fine cape blazing like a torch as he launched himself at a goon. Sulley followed, his own cape billowing behind him. He didn't have his armor, but he had his might, and he wasn't slowing down. A goon landed a solid hit on her shoulder, and Snow White turned back to the fight with renewed ferocity. Between slams and parries with her stave, she saw Tiana and Rapunzel arrive and was amused to see Rapunzel wielding her hairpin and ready to get stabby. Last of all, Hades sauntered over, a blue fireball in one hand and a glass of something bubbly in the other.

"Some party," he said glumly. "I can't believe I had to miss the Cha-Cha Slide for this." He did brighten up when he started fighting a goon, Snow White noticed.

Perhaps he pretended he didn't enjoy the fray, but he couldn't hide his smile when he was in the midst of it.

Snow White took more hits on her shoulder and hip while she fought the goon; she was just too distracted by everything happening—and by keeping an eye on the Prince, whose eyes glowed green as he tried to fight his way free of the improvised prison the forest had provided. Her skirts blunted the blow of the goon's attempts to strike her legs with its halberd, and she'd soon reduced it to a pile of glimmering shards.

Finally able to draw a breath in the tight bodice, she surveyed the destruction tearing across the once-beautiful garden. The Fractured goons had trampled through the flower beds, and Sulley had landed on his back on a rosebush, leaving him wincing with thorns riddling his backside. Stitch, his molecular structure altered to make him as big as a bear, had accidentally slammed into several cherry trees, knocking them over like dominoes. Rapunzel was doing her best with her hairpin but obviously missed her frying pan. She'd slung her hair over a branch and was ricocheting off trees with her feet, stabbing the goon with each swing.

Hades refused to put down his drink, but his aim with one hand was still excellent, and Snow White kept having to stamp out little fires that sprang up as his flames exploded against his goon and sent sparks swirling around the garden.

"Not sure which party is more boring," he said to no one in particular. "The one with the dancing and politeness or the one with the fighting and rabid badgers."

"Why, they're not rabid!" Snow White said. "They're just drooling a little!"

As for Tiana, she had her bag at the ready and was slinging dangerous potions at the goons whenever they turned their backs.

"Never going to a ball without a weapon again," she muttered between throws. "Even really good biscuit recipes aren't worth this!"

The goons couldn't stand against the combined might of the Guardians and the flora and fauna of the forest. One by one, they exploded with that familiar sound of breaking glass. At last, the garden was quiet and still, devoid of purple energy. A turtle stumbled out of the forest and looked around, blinking with surprise to discover he'd missed the all the action. The

animals didn't quite know what to do, and the bear ambled toward Sulley as if asking for a fight.

"No, I'm good," Sulley said, hands up. "Nice claws, though. You'd give me a run for top Scarer."

"Thank you all so much," Snow White said, her voice ringing loud in the absence of battle. "I can't tell you how much I appreciate your coming when I called. You did a simply marvelous job, and I'm so proud of you. If only I had some way to repay you . . ." She trailed off, and the squirrels twirled their tails in anticipation. "Oh! There's ever so much food in the castle, just up those stairs. I imagine that if the bear goes first, the people inside will run away, and you can eat your fill. Just don't give yourselves a tummy ache!"

Twittering and tweeting and squeaking and snuffling, the forest creatures charged up the stone steps to the balcony and poured through the velvet curtains. Human screams and gasps rang through the night, along with thunderous footsteps.

"I suspect the castle staff won't like that," Snow White said to herself, realizing her error. "I'm going to have to apologize, once everything is settled."

Only the deer remained, holding the Prince hostage with their antlers. Snow White walked over to him and pulled the vines from his mouth.

"You foul, nasty little beast," he growled. "How dare you—"

She put the vine back. "Tia, do you have some more of that potion? He's been poisoned by the Queen."

Tiana frowned and dug through her bag. "I haven't had time to make more yet, but this garden should have everything I need, now that we've got plenty of jewels."

She spread out her ingredients on top of a nearby stone wall and began to work, and Snow White turned back to the Guardians. "And thank you all, too. I'm so sorry to have interrupted the ball."

"You were being attacked by goons in a garden," Rapunzel said with a shrug. "I think we can put down the petits fours and do our jobs. Although . . . do you think maybe there will be any left after the bear eats his fill? Because those were really, really great petits fours."

"Bears can't open bottles." Hades drained his glass. "Which is why I prefer animals without opposable thumbs." He chucked the glass over his shoulder, and Snow White flinched when it shattered. The sound reminded her of a goon exploding. She swiped her hand to the side, and a patch of dandelions sprung up over the glass.

"Okay," Tiana said. "I think it's ready. Let's heal your boyfriend."

The Prince growled through the vines, "I'm not her anything, she's a hideous little fool—"

Tiana raised a disgusted eyebrow at his outburst. "That's enough out of you. Stitch? Sulley? A little help?"

The stags backed away, and Stitch and Sulley each took the Prince by an arm. He thrashed and grunted in their grasp as Tiana approached, potion in hand.

"You'll never win," he hissed. "You're all pathetic and miserable, Snow White most of all. I'd never love her, not in a thousand years, not if she was the last girl left in the world. Ridiculous. Stupid. Boring. Useless. Powerless. Helpless."

Snow White twitched a finger, and the vines silenced him. She knew the words weren't real, and yet they stung. She'd heard such things from the Queen often enough. Part of her wanted to turn away and cry, to admit that he wasn't necessarily wrong.

And yet . . .

No.

She stepped past Tiana and up to the Prince, the stags shifting their bodies away to give her room. He twitched and growled low in his throat, green eyes filled with hate.

"Those are lies, and you can't hurt me," she told him. "And neither can the Queen you serve."

She stepped away.

"Tia, your turn."

16

Tiana walked over, and the stags moved to let her into their circle.

"Here we go. I hope this works. Snow, can you help him open up?"

Snow White pulled the vines from the Prince's mouth—or, rather, she urged the vines to release him. Before he could insult her again, she pinched his nose and Tiana poured the potion down, getting most of it between his lips.

"We're getting pretty good at this," she said, grinning at Snow White.

As the potion did its work, the acidic green washed out of the Prince's eyes, leaving them that dreamy, sunny blue.

"How are you?" Snow White asked nervously.

He smiled at her. "Snow White, what a beautiful vision! But—why am I caught up in these vines? And—the stags . . ."

"You can let go now," Snow White said, tapping her finger gently on a jasmine flower. The vines uncurled and retreated to their trellis, climbing back up and settling with a sigh of relief as the roots coiled back into the earth. At her nod, the stags bowed and backed away. "You were ensorcelled, I'm afraid. Poisoned. Do you remember anything?"

The Prince looked around at the wreck of his garden and blinked in confusion. "I was called away to attend to the acrobats—some problem with a camel, I think—and then I joined you outside, and I bent to pluck a flower the exact shade as your lips, and a bee stung me—" He frowned, then gasped. "It's as if I said horrible things to you, my lady. Things I didn't mean. It felt as if they came from somewhere, from someone else. Please tell me that was some nightmare, and that you didn't have to hear such lies from my lips."

Snow White sighed. "I knew it wasn't you. The Queen's poison is insidious. But it's gone now. The only real loss here is the beauty of your garden, but maybe . . ." She closed her eyes and knelt, placing her palms in the grass as her skirts billowed around her. She could feel all the tiny roots and worms and growing things, all tangled up beautifully underground, and she sent her love and goodwill out through that network, thanking the plants and urging them to take what they needed of her energy. When she opened her eyes, the garden was swelling with life, buds blooming and trees righting themselves as if by magic. She was a little tired and dizzy, but it was worth it to help something grow.

"Are you doing that?" the Prince asked. "Are you some sort of goddess?"

"Oh, no!" Snow White laughed. "Just someone who loves the forest very much, and the garden is simply a tame forest, isn't it? With time, it will all grow back, more beautiful than ever."

The Prince held out his hand and helped her stand. "You are a revelation, my lady."

"Please do call me Snow White. I told you so before, but . . . well . . ."

"The poison," he supplied.

"Yes, the poison. Oh, I just wish things weren't so very strange now. I'm wishing—"

"You're wishing?"

"For something . . ."

"For something?"

"For something *normal*. I'd like to stay here and get to know you better, but we have to go stop the Queen. And I thought perhaps you could help us, but now I see that she'll use you against me, if she can. She'll use you to hurt me. And you'll need to stay here and defend your own kingdom, because wherever there are Fractured goons"—she walked a few steps toward the forest and reached up to hold a leaf with a single purple crack running through it—"there will be trouble."

"So you're not staying?" His blue eyes pled with her, and her heart tugged her toward him, and she longed to be back in his arms, waltzing without a care.

"I can't stay, not now. But know that where I'm going and what I'm doing—it's so that perhaps we can meet again one day, with no poison and no fighting, and dance again." She looked up to the castle. "I'll ask the animals to leave the ballroom, and then we'll have to go, too."

"But it's nighttime! The forest could be dangerous—"

Snow White chuckled sadly. "Oh, it definitely is dangerous. But the Queen knows where we are, and we can't risk staying here and bringing yet more trouble to your doorstep. I promise we'll be back, after we succeed."

"I'm not doubting you, of course, but what if . . . what if this evil queen overpowers you?"

She stuck out her chin. "If we don't succeed, there won't be anything to come back to."

Snow White led the way toward the castle, the Prince hurrying to catch up with her and the Guardians trailing behind. She called out to the animals at the buffet table, thanking them for their help and asking them to please return to the forest. With food-smeared faces and sleepy yawns, they ran and skittered and bounded out, the bear waddling by last of all, licking pudding off his nose. The poor turtle still waited at the bottom step as the rest of the beasts hurried over him, one of the raccoons using his shell as a stair.

The Guardians separated, returning to the baths to change back into their far more comfortable and fight-ready costumes. Snow White had often dreamed of wearing a ball gown back when she was a scullery maid, but she sighed with relief once she was free of the movement-limiting skirts and insufficient satin slippers and back in the outfit that Mickey's magic had crafted just to suit her. Her pickaxe seemed to tingle at her touch, a new flower sprouting near the blade.

"No more parties unless we're fully armed," Rapunzel said, hugging her frying pan. Her feet were bare again, but Snow White could see where the slippers had bitten into her poor ankles, leaving blisters.

"Then you're going to need a big purse," Tiana said, patting her own bag in place. "Even the most generous pockets can't fit cast-iron cookware."

Back upstairs, they regrouped with the others. The ballroom was a riot of busy servants trying to clean up the wreckage left behind by a hungry bear, but Snow White didn't see the Prince anywhere. Sure, they'd said one goodbye, but she wanted another. With Fractured Magic taking over, there was a chance she'd never see him again. She dragged her feet as they neared the castle gate, constantly looking back over her shoulder.

Finally he appeared, hurrying toward them with a picnic basket over one arm.

"I hoped you hadn't left yet," he told her.

"And I hoped you were hoping that," she said with a smile.

"It's not much, but we packed up whatever the animals didn't destroy—and what the cooks had planned for breakfast." The Prince handed her the basket, which was heavier than anticipated and smelled of warm bread. "Hopefully this will help you on your journey. I'll be waiting for you to return."

The Prince bowed, and Snow White curtsied, and Hades shouted, "Kiss already!"

At that, they both straightened and blushed, waving as they parted ways.

When Snow White and the Guardians arrived at the castle, it had seemed like a dream, like it was made of spun clouds of sugary perfection. As they left, Snow White was demoralized to see purple cracks inching up the foundation and purple streaks in the ivy climbing up the walls. Had they brought the Fractured Magic with them, dooming this place to a faster descent into chaos? Guilt made her shoulders hunch up as she realized that wherever she went, she brought darkness. It wasn't her fault, of course; the Queen was responsible for using the Fractured Mirror to set this world on a path of destruction. But that path was following Snow White's footsteps, creeping behind her like the Huntsman, leaving a trail of purple cracks and carnage in her wake.

She walked faster after that, leading the others

down from the castle's promontory and into a foggy, deserted valley that she was quite certain hadn't been there before.

"Nice place," Hades said, "Reminds me of this lovely crypt where I used to hang out and chill. Just vast swaths of emptiness, you know?"

The path zigged and zagged between steep cliffs. There were no growing green things or animals, just jagged boulders and malformed, twisted dead trees. An occasional thump from overhead made them all stumble back as rocks tumbled down the slopes and smashed against the dirt.

"We need to camp for the night," Rapunzel said with a jaw-cracking yawn. "And I'm not saying that because those slippers gave me blisters."

"This place . . . I don't trust it." Snow White looked all around. "It feels like we're trapped. I think we should keep going until we're out of the canyon."

"But if we don't get sleep, we won't be able to fight if we're attacked," Sulley pointed out.

"But if we get crushed in a rockslide while we sleep, we won't be able to live," Tiana said firmly. "There's no place to take shelter. We have to keep going, just a little longer."

And so they trudged endlessly through the darkness,

dodging falling rocks and jumping at every dead tree that pierced the dirt and loomed ahead through the mist like a wicked witch. Snow White yawned and stumbled on a rock, her fall stopped only by Sulley's giant paws catching her shoulders. It seemed as if they were going nowhere, and each step filled the air with more rock dust and hopelessness.

"Dry," Stitch said, his tongue hanging out and looking far less slobbery than usual.

Snow White poked around in the picnic basket and handed out bright red apples, hoping the juicy sweetness would keep everyone going through the night. When that didn't suffice, she passed out grapes and strawberries and tea cakes. They were eating through their stores, but she seemed to recall hearing once that an army marched on its stomach. If they couldn't sleep, at least they could eat. The banquet and its glorious plenty seemed like something that had happened to someone else, somewhere else, years ago, in a dream. If Snow White thought too hard about the deliciously fizzy punch, her mouth started watering.

"Are we wandering in circles?" Sulley finally asked. "I'm pretty sure I've seen that twisted stump before. It looks like this guy I know named Randall."

"If we're wandering in circles, it's because this canyon is a circle," Tiana said. "Maybe there's a way up we've been missing because we've been so busy focusing on the ground?"

Snow White looked up at the steep cliff walls, wishing it were a bright day with blue skies and balmy breezes. Even with the moon's blue light, the stone faces of the canyon were a jumble of light and shadow.

But there—something moved.

She squinted and saw dark creatures rustling.

"Vultures!" she said, pointing. "Why, there are vultures up there! And they don't look nice at all."

"That's because they want to eat you," Hades said. "It's the circle of life."

"I think I see a path up there, too." Rapunzel pointed. "If I squint just right."

Sulley looked up, considering it. "Was it made for goats?"

"Goats?" Stitch perked up. "To eat?"

"No, don't eat any goats," Snow White said. "But maybe you could lead us up the path? You seem like the best climber."

Stitch walked to the wall and clung to it like a bug. He skittered around until he found a place where he could stand upright. "Yep, good climber," he said. "Found it." Sure enough, there was a little path, mostly comprising ledges. Rapunzel went next, then Snow White, Tiana, Hades, and at last, Sulley.

"I don't think this is a path," the big monster grumbled as he clung to the side of the mountain, digging his claws into the rock as he edged his way sideways up the trail.

"It is now," Tiana said firmly. "And it's our only way out of here."

So many times, Snow White almost slipped and fell. She had to hold on to her pickaxe with one hand and cling to the mountain with the other, and she promised herself that if she got through the night alive and uncrushed by falling rocks or by falling *on* rocks, she would rig some sort of scabbard to carry her weapon on her back. Every time she tripped or slipped, Tiana was there to help steady her with a kind word, or Rapunzel stopped and looked back to encourage her.

She simply wasn't made for this kind of adventuring— this kind of danger. Or, at least, she hadn't been before this. Just a few days earlier, facing such a challenge, she might've been tempted to give up hope. Just like that day so long ago, when she'd run into the forest and seen only dangerous shadows and sharp teeth, and nearly given in to her terror.

And yet here she was, pushed to her limit, pushed *beyond* her limit . . . but she continued. Was it the Stellar Magic, amplifying her own powers? Was it the camaraderie and support of the Guardians? Or was there perhaps something inside her, something new and only now beginning to bloom, that gave her a strength and resilience she'd never dreamed of?

Whatever it was, in that endless night, clinging to a bare stone wall far above the cold, hard floor of a haunted valley and witnessed by stars and hungry vultures, she was glad of it.

Finally, finally, Rapunzel dragged herself up onto flat ground, then turned to give Snow White her hand. Snow White tossed her pickaxe over the edge and climbed up on her hands and knees, her legs too tired to hold her up for a moment longer. She immediately turned around to help Tiana up, realizing that even if she couldn't go on for her own sake, she could go on for her friends'. Once everyone was off the trail and far from the treacherous ledge, they looked around at their new surroundings.

"Well, this is better," Hades said, dusting off his

hands and then setting them on fire with blue flames as if to cleanse them of the canyon's dust. "It's so nice to be looking at jagged mountains instead of jagged cliffs."

Snow White gasped when she saw a familiar sight. "There it is! The Queen's castle!"

Craggy dark gray peaks loomed over everything, piercing the sky like claws. Just a little farther on, the hard brown dirt gave way to scrub grass, then bushes, then sturdy pine trees leading down to the river that formed the moat around the Queen's castle. It was finally within reach!

"We have to hurry—" Snow White began.

"We have to sleep," Tiana said firmly.

"Stitch is already out." Sulley stood over the blue alien, who was on his back, eyes closed, tongue hanging out, snoring.

"Just for a few hours," Tiana promised. "Not long enough for the Fractured Magic to devour the world, just long enough for me to stop hallucinating that the big rocks are beignets." She looked around at each of them, and her expression softened. "And I need to make some more healing potions, because y'all need 'em. Snow, you took damage in that fight. You should've said something."

Snow White rubbed her shoulder where the goon's first arrow had landed a solid hit. "Oh, well, there was so much going on. We needed to get somewhere safe."

"This is safe for now." Tiana handed her a bottle of healing potion, and she drank just enough to send that warmth swirling through her. Her shoulder stopped its dreary ache, and her legs felt just a little less rubbery. Satisfied, she handed the rest of her potion on to Rapunzel.

"Ohhhh, my blistered heels say thanks." Rapunzel wiggled her toes with a huge sigh of relief.

Fortunately, there was an overhang nearby that offered some protection from the elements, and they were all eager to set up camp. It wasn't cozy, but it was something. Snow White couldn't get comfortable—no pillow, no blanket, just hard stone. But even with the effects of the healing potion, she couldn't escape the fact that her mind, body, and heart had been pushed to their limits, and soon she would fall into a sleep as rocky as the ground under her head. Nearby, Tiana hummed to herself as she hurriedly mixed potions and restocked her bag. The last thing Snow White saw as her eyes closed was Hades sitting on a boulder, pinching his blue hair so the flames would die down to a light simmer.

The next thing she knew, a huge crash shook her awake as Hades said, "Uh-oh."

She sat up straight, reaching for her weapon.

If the god of death was worried, they were seriously in trouble.

—◇—

17

Snow White was on her feet in an instant, her pickaxe in hand. "What's wrong?"

Hades stood right under the edge of the overhang, looking out. It was dawn, but the sort of dawn that promised the day would never be anything other than gray and wet and miserable, as if the sun had given up before it even began to rise.

"A storm's rolling in," he said without turning around.

"Why, what's so worrisome about that?"

He looked at her in a pitying sort of way. "When

your least favorite brother is the god of the sky and has a thing for lightning bolts, let's just say a storm takes on a different meaning. And this is gonna be one mean storm. Can't you feel it making your eyebrows stand on end?"

Snow White didn't sense anything in her eyebrows, but there was definitely a feeling in the air—as if it were alive and waiting.

Hearing their voices, the Guardians woke up one by one, stretching and grimacing as they clutched various body parts that had grown sore or numb after several hours on solid rock.

"Guess it's going to be a soggy day," Rapunzel said, holding her frying pan over her head experimentally to see if it would provide any protection from the elements.

"The sooner we're into the forest, the sooner we'll have cover from the trees." Tiana tucked her hair up in a kerchief she'd pulled from her bag. "Everybody ready?"

Once they'd finally gotten Stitch awake and Snow White had passed out some of the petits fours from the ball as breakfast, they abandoned their outcropping and ran for the relative safety of the forest. Thunder roiled overhead, and Snow White kept waiting to feel the patter of raindrops.

Crash!

A bolt of lightning struck the ground just ahead of them, the world exploding in a burst of white-hot light. Snow White skidded to a stop, nearly running into Hades.

"This feels familiar in the worst possible way," he muttered.

As if on cue, rain fell like a box of rocks, instantly drenching Snow White and making her pickaxe slippery in her grasp.

"It's just rain!" she shouted. "Just a storm. We need to keep going!"

"Oh, you sweet, innocent nincompoop." Hades pointed up to a promontory, a pitch-black spire rising against the tumultuous gray clouds.

A figure stood there—a man, well-muscled, monumental and solid, bearded and holding a bolt of lightning. He was bigger than life, his features snarling with rage.

As lightning again rent the sky, Snow White saw that he was also Fractured, crackling with purple energy.

"Betrayer!" the figure said, pointing at Hades.

Another figure appeared beside him, a beefy man with a fin where his hair should've been. "Murderer!" he said, also pointing at Hades. The third figure was a woman with a huge hairdo shaped like a beehive who shouted, "Traitor!" Last of all came a figure that might've been a handsome young hero, if he hadn't been Fractured and sparking violet.

"Bad uncle!" he said.

But Hades just rolled his eyes. "Ooh, yes. So scary. I'm being faced with my darkest fears, having my worst qualities used against me by my jerk family. Oh, look at me having a crisis of conscience! I should've been a better guy, huh?" He blew a raspberry and turned to Snow White and the Guardians. "Look, this isn't deep. We just have to fight these goons. I know that's not my brother Zeus or my other brother, Poseidon, or my sister Hestia, and I know that's not my idiot nephew Hercules, and even if it was, I have literally no problem destroying them in this world or any other world. I would relish it, in fact."

Rapunzel turned to Snow White, the rain sleeking her hair down into a puddle of gold. "I think he's putting on an act. Even if they are his fake family, that's got to hurt."

"Betrayer!" Fractured Zeus said again, launching an illuminating bolt of lightning to the ground, right where Hades was standing. The Guardians scattered before it struck, and Snow White dropped the picnic basket to leap and roll away, coming up with her pickaxe held high.

Hades rolled his shoulders and cracked his neck, the blue fire of his hair burning brighter despite the rain and trailing down his arms to his hands, where two swirling fireballs formed.

"I know you are, but what am I?" he shouted.

With a roar, he launched both fireballs, one after the other, right at the Fractured version of his brother Zeus. The first one missed, but the second one struck home in a shower of sparks.

He looked back to the Guardians. "Come on, everyone! If you can fight all those other goons, you can fight these punks. They're not actually gods! I should know—we can smell our own. And all I smell is ozone."

Two more fireballs appeared in his hands, and he charged for the promontory, launching them at the Fractured versions of his brothers as he leapt from crag to crag. Snow White envied his surety, recalling how conflicted she'd felt fighting her Fractured friends and then how much she'd hated using her powers against the poisoned Prince. She wasn't sure whom she should fight first—until Fractured goons appeared, marching up from the forest. She could barely see through the sheeting rain, but it helped that the goons crackled with electricity, their purple glow giving away their position.

"Stitch and Rapunzel, you head for the—for Hades's family," Tiana said. "Snow White and Sulley, let's take out these normal goons."

"Big fish," Stitch said, scrambling up the jagged peaks toward the god with the fish fin on his head. Seeing him coming, the Fractured god lumbered down the mountain, swinging a trident.

"That's Poseidon," Hades shouted in between throwing fireballs and dodging lightning. "And there's definitely something fishy about him. And not just the smell."

"Oh, wow. Your sister has great hair!" Rapunzel exclaimed as she hitched her own hair up over her arm like a coil of rope and climbed toward the third figure.

"Hestia, goddess of hearth and home," Hades explained. Then, louder, "Home, as in where she should've stayed!"

The fourth family member—Hercules—had disappeared, but Fractured Poseidon and Hestia scrambled down the mountain to meet their foes. Snow White turned her attention to the regular goons swiftly approaching. The first time she'd faced them, she'd been scared, but with each fight, she grew more confident. This didn't feel life-and-death anymore; it felt like her job, like something she was meant to do. And like something she was good at. She planted her feet and swung her pickaxe, and it slammed into the nearest goon with a meaty *thunk.*

Every fight, she was learning, was an odd mix of focusing on the enemy in front of you and taking tiny moments, whenever possible, to assess the battle and see what might be sneaking up on you next. This fight was made even more hectic by the pounding rain, crashing lightning, and the ground rumbling underfoot with each crack of thunder. On one side, they faced the jagged black mountains, and on the other, the cliff that led down, down, down to the canyon where they'd already been trapped once—and that offered the sort of bone-crushing fall that even Tiana's potions might not be able to heal. Snow White's every sense was on high alert as she ducked and dodged and struck again and again with her pickaxe. The goon landed a hit on her ribs with its axe, making her stumble back, but she found a renewed energy and fought on.

"Gettin' good over there, Snow," Sulley said as he traded punches with a beefy goon.

"Oh, well, thank you. . . ." She trailed off as she ducked under a slash and took advantage of the goon's imbalance to whip her pickaxe around and knock it off its feet.

"You're doing great. I can't believe how far you've come in just a couple of days. You swing that pickaxe like it's part of you."

Despite the fact that she was fighting for her life in a storm, Snow White blushed. "That's kind of you to say."

"It's true. Own it. You're supposed to feel proud when you do a good job. Oof!" The beefy goon socked Sulley in the stomach, and he went silent as he redoubled his onslaught, his yellow armor lit up and crackling with power.

With Snow White's next slash, her goon exploded in a burst of purple light. Without even pausing to celebrate, she smoothly pivoted to face the next goon, already ducking under its first sword jab to hack right into its side. It felt like a dance, albeit a very different dance from the waltz she'd shared with the Prince. She was just as adept at both activities, much to her surprise. It wasn't so much that she enjoyed fighting goons, and yet . . . in a way, she did. It brought out a fierce joy in her, a sense of rightness. She wasn't just fighting against, she was fighting *for*—for her friends, for her forest, for her world. And fighting alongside the Guardians gave her a feeling of camaraderie, of community, that she'd been looking for all her life.

Her next goon exploded, and when she spun for the next one, she found only Sulley breathing heavily, one hand to his stomach.

"I don't know about you, but I'm ready for that healing potion," he said with a grin.

"Betrayer!"

The voice rang out, echoing off the mountains, and everyone looked up to where Hades fought with the Fractured version of his very much not beloved brother.

"Why hasn't he exploded yet?" Snow White asked Sulley.

"Some goons are more powerful than others," Sulley explained. "Like . . . bosses. I guess that guy's a boss." He thought about it for a second. "I sure hope I never have to face the Fractured version of my boss. Mr. Waternoose has way too many legs. And eyes. And teeth." He shivered, throwing rainwater like a wet dog.

Rapunzel, Stitch, and Tiana joined Sulley and Snow White, and they all watched Hades grapple with Fractured Zeus. Maybe Hades said his brother couldn't hurt him, but he certainly seemed to be upset with this evil copy of the real Zeus.

"You can't tell me what to do!" he shouted at it, even though all it could say in response was, "Betrayer!"

Snow White scanned the area, looking for more enemies. Fractured Poseidon and Hestia were gone, Hercules had disappeared, and no more regular goons were waiting to fight. But—

"Oh, no! Our picnic basket!" she said.

There it sat, overturned in the rain; all their delicious food would soon be either soaked or washed away. So far from the cottage and the Prince's castle, and with the forest overrun with Fractured Magic, food would be hard to come by. Snow White ran over to where the fight had originally started and knelt to gather up the apples, grapes, berries, and hunks of cheese that had fallen out of the basket when she'd dropped it. The petits fours, sadly, had melted into little pink puddles, but the rest of the food wasn't hurt, so she tucked everything back in the basket as swiftly as she could.

"Snow, look out!" Sulley shouted.

When she looked up, she saw the Fractured godling, Hades's nephew Hercules, pushing a giant boulder from a ledge high up the mountain. With a horrifying rumble, it began to roll, immediately picking up speed as it descended. As she stood to run, her foot caught on a stone, the purple-cracked ground surging up around her ankle to trap it completely. She tripped, her pickaxe flying from her hands to clatter on the ground, out of reach. She struggled to stand and tugged and tugged, trying to free herself as the boulder bounded and rolled down the mountain, directly toward her.

It was no use. Perhaps she could speak to the forest and the earth, but this stone belonged entirely to the Fractured magic now, and it had her exactly where it wanted her.

"You think I'm going to let you get away?" Hades screamed at Zeus. "You think I'm going to let you win just because you threatened some girl with a marble?"

The other Guardians were running toward her, but it was like they were in slow motion, the entire world in perfect clarity as Snow White watched the boulder get closer and closer as it built speed. They weren't going to make it, though—they were too slow and too far away.

Only Hades could stop it with his fireballs, but Hades couldn't tear his attention away from his nemesis—or the stupid, fake version of his nemesis.

"Hades!" Snow White called. "Help!"

He looked at her and shrugged.

"Sorry, Snow, but revenge comes first."

18

Hades was the god of death, and every moment of his life reminded him of that fact. He hadn't chosen this path, hadn't asked to be a baby who often caught on fire and singed whoever was holding him up, but that was his lot in life. Or death. He couldn't really draw the line between them anymore.

The one thing he knew for sure was that his brother Zeus was the golden boy who was just handed everything good in the universe for literally no reason. Zeus wasn't smarter or stronger or better looking than Hades. He hadn't fought for the right to rule Olympus and be the king of the gods. It was all an accident of birth. Even

Poseidon had a better lot—the entire ocean! Most of the planet! All the lobster he could eat!

And all Hades got was a three-headed dog and the ability to make any room smell like rotten eggs.

At least, that was what it felt like most of the time.

And that was why he couldn't just stop the fight to help some random human girl he'd just met. He'd waited an eternity to get one over on Zeus, and now was his chance.

He leapt up the last few crags until at last he stood on equal footing with his brother. Sure, this version was purple and crackling and had empty white eyes, but Hades was accustomed to his brother changing forms. Zeus could be a peacock or a bull, so why not pretend he was a Fractured just to torture Hades some more? It was plausible, and the way this guy was fighting, it seemed more and more likely.

"Betrayer," Zeus said, and Hades took great joy in rearing back, his fist wreathed in flames, to punch his brother right in his handsome jaw.

But Zeus didn't respond, didn't spit out a tooth or whine or fall over. He just kept fighting, pulling a lightning bolt out of the air and trying to stab Hades in the chest with it.

"At least you're not trying to stab me in the back

this time, huh?" Hades said, swatting the bolt aside and sending it clattering down the cliff.

With a grunt, he sent his hair flames into overdrive and headbutted Zeus, which caused a bright burst of purple crackles. Just a few more hits, and this Fractured jerk would be gone. Unless it was the real Zeus, and then maybe Hades could get rid of him once and for all.

"Hades, please!" Snow White called again.

This time, he didn't bother to respond. She was a mortal, her life a bare whisper compared to his roar. When she showed up in the Underworld, he'd give her a nice spot in the Elysian Fields, maybe, in apology. He wouldn't let anyone torture her with hot coals. He would let her rub Cerberus's belly. That was pretty generous, for a god.

As it turned out, his curiosity about becoming a Guardian meant nothing when compared to his lifelong need to supplant his brother.

"I've been waiting a long time for this," he said, and blue fire shot down his arm, gathering in his hand as he prepared for the killing blow.

A thousand pounds of death rolled down the mountain, and Snow White was helpless to stop it. Her pickaxe couldn't save her, her friends couldn't save her, the Prince couldn't save her, and even the Guardians couldn't save her. They couldn't reach her in time. It was all up to Hades, and Hades had definitely chosen otherwise.

But as she watched in frozen horror, Sulley picked up Stitch by the back of his spacesuit, reared back, and launched the alien at the boulder like he was throwing a javelin. As Stitch flew through the air, he burned with orange fire, the rain sizzling and turning to steam the second it touched him. He slammed into the boulder with his fist, and it shattered into a cloud of gravel and dust that rained down around Snow White as she ducked, arms over her head.

The Guardians immediately surrounded her. Sulley pried back the rocks with his mighty paws, freeing Snow White's ankle with a mighty crack and a shower of pebbles, and Tiana handed her a healing potion, which she drank down in one big gulp.

Rapunzel slung an arm around her shoulders. "You okay? That was pretty scary."

"Rock," Snow White managed, still a bit stunned as the potion did its work.

"Rock," Stitch agreed, wiggling his fingers and wincing.

"I can't believe Hades just let that happen," Tiana said, arms crossed.

"When I get my hands on that selfish, irresponsible menace—" Sulley began.

"It's okay." Snow White stood. "I'm fine now."

"That's not how a Guardian—or even a potential Guardian—should act. Mickey needs to know." Tiana watched as Hades took down Fractured Zeus with a massive fireball. As the goon crackled into crystals, Hades did a victory dance, oblivious to the drama happening elsewhere.

"Can't wait to brag about that at the next family reunion!" he crowed, right up until a crackling purple arrow thwacked into his foot—or where his foot would've been, if it hadn't been partially smoke. "Oh no you did not!" Hades shouted, his flames roaring upward in a cloud of steam. "I'm sending you back to the kids' table, Herc the Jerk!"

"Oh, yeah, Mickey will definitely find out about it," Rapunzel said, moving wet hair out of her face. "But look at it this way—he hasn't contacted us yet, so he must trust that we can do this on our own." Pascal crawled out of her hair, a frosty shade of turquoise, and shook himself off, his eyes wobbling in every direction.

"Come back, you little coward!" Hades screeched as

he hurled fireballs at his nephew's doppelgänger. "Maybe your father won't discipline you, but I will! We don't!" Fireball. "Throw!" Fireball. "Boulders!" Fireball. "At ladies!" Fireball. "Except maybe Hera sometimes."

Fractured Hercules exploded into purple shards, and Hades pumped his fist and did another victory dance, which included a moonwalk.

"Fine. But we tell Mickey when we're done," Tiana grumbled. "Let's get out of here."

Sulley handed Snow White her pickaxe, and she picked the picnic basket back up off the ground. She was shaking, and not just from being soaked and chilly. Tiana led the group toward the trees, and they all kept looking back to the mountains. The storm was moving off, the rain easing to a drizzle as the sun broke through the clouds.

"I don't know why you guys get so upset," Hades said, inspecting his nails. "Blah blah blah, the purple people, feelings. Not such a big deal."

"Well, let's just say you looked pretty upset when you were fighting that guy with the beard." Tiana smirked.

"Just because he can grow a beard doesn't mean he's better than me!" Hades shrieked, his hair shooting up like a volcano.

"Yeah, you're right," Rapunzel said. "You seem to be very comfortable talking about your family. Not upset at all. I mean, I can relate. My mom . . . well, she's not my real mom, but—I understand family problems. And I don't pretend I don't have them."

Sulley held out his pinky and thumb and held his hand up to the side of his face. "Hello, people who are calm and collected and have good self-control? Do you have room for one more? Because Hades is joining you."

"What's he doing?" Snow White whispered to Rapunzel.

"I have no idea," Rapunzel whispered back.

"Telephone," Stitch said, as if it were obvious.

"That's not what a telephone looks like," Tiana said.

"What's a telephone?" Rapunzel and Snow White both asked.

Sulley's brow scrunched down. "It's a piece of technology that—" He shook his head. "You know what? Let's just forget about it and focus on getting away from Mount Sibling Rivalry."

Hades let out a tired sigh. "It's not sibling rivalry, you know. We were just born this way. Zeus gets everything, I get nothing, Poseidon gets something in between. No matter what I do, I am still the worst brother. They don't give out gold stars for doing a great job of ruling the Underworld, you know?"

"Oh, but I'm sure you're wonderful at what you do," Snow White said.

"You're awfully forgiving to a guy who was going to let you die." Rapunzel shook her head. "I mean, rude."

"Well, it's easy to let emotions take over," Snow White allowed. "If I'd been a little more careful and a little less trusting, you all wouldn't have been caught up in a fight in the Prince's garden. I just wanted so badly to live my dream. So I guess I can understand if Hades lost control—"

"Oh, I was in complete control," Hades said darkly. "God brains work differently than human brains. I can't even apologize, because that would be a lie, and I don't care enough to lie. I'd do it again. Shattering the fake version of my brother was the best thing I've ever done."

"Then that's why you should become a Guardian," Snow White said. "Because maybe then you could really do something better with your life."

"Afterlife."

"Existence," she corrected. "I think you just need a purpose."

Hades snorted sadly. "Yeah, because ruling the entire Underworld and all the billions of souls therein just isn't quite enough for an overachiever like me. Maybe I just need something more than a tiny little nothing job like that."

"It's always hard when someone says you're not good enough—" she started.

"Good enough?" he barked. "You have to be *good* before you can be good enough. I never even got that far!"

"It's still hard."

Snow White patted his arm, surprised at how it felt both solid and like smoke and was feverishly warm. His hand landed on hers, a brief, hot squeeze, and then he snorted and strode ahead of everyone else.

"*Pfft.* Whatever. Glad you're not dead, I guess. That would mean even more paperwork for me. Not that I care."

Snow White giggled to herself. Hades was a complicated . . . whatever he was . . . but perhaps she'd hit too close to home, bringing up his lack of a true purpose.

They entered the forest, the temperature cooler under cover of the fluffy green fir branches, and Snow White finally felt like she could relax a little. Sure, the woods were showing signs of being Fractured, with purple cracks in the tree trunks and purple veins running through the leaves, but underneath that sickness was still a forest, an extension of her forest, and it was as happy to see her as she was to see it. The birds called to each other from tree to tree as she passed by, sounding like excited gossips with big news, and soon squirrels and chipmunks rushed out to bounce on the ends of branches, chittering excitedly at her. The forest and its creatures . . . they needed her help. Along with the Guardians, she would drive out the Fractured Magic and return the forest to the way it should've been, a healthy and thriving place. She waved to the squirrels and scratched chipmunks under their chins as she passed. Rabbits hopped out to gaze at her in wonder and raccoons blinked sleepily from their holes in old tree trunks.

"We'll fix it," she promised them. "Why, we're on our way to stop it!"

This part of the forest had no trails, and she took the lead as they sought the least challenging path through the tangled underbrush. The vines tried to part before her—at least, the ones that weren't already poisoned. She felt as if the land itself was guiding her toward the Queen's castle, toward the Fractured Mirror poisoning her world. Every leaf and blade of grass glittered with rain, and as the sun came out and warmed the world, a dense fog rose up from the ground, making it even harder to press forward.

"Are you sure you know where you're going?" Hades asked. "Because it all looks about the same to me."

"It's not." Snow White put a hand to a tree, and it was as if the tree spoke to her, assuring her she was headed the correct way. "The forest is taking us right where we need to go. It wouldn't lead us wrong."

"Plenty of things in this world have led us wrong," he grumbled under his breath.

"Guy who's jealous of his brother says what?" Sulley muttered.

"What?" Hades asked, annoyed.

Sulley grinned. "Exactly."

It felt like forever until the forest began to thin out, but Snow White started to see glimpses of a familiar castle.

"There it is, up ahead!" She pushed aside the branches of a thick fir tree, revealing the red spires of the castle she'd once loved but had grown to despise. "We're almost there!"

As soon as the way was free, she broke into a run. She was tired, sore, and sleepy, but it felt so good to see her goal finally in sight. The Fractured Magic had put every obstacle possible in their way, but it had failed. The castle was there, no longer able to hide, which meant that the evil queen and the Fractured Mirror were within their grasp. She ran faster, desperate to close the distance, to fight the final fight and save her friends and set her world free of the magic that was poisoning it.

But wait.

There was the castle . . . but where was the bridge?

She knew that there had been one over the shallow green moat, a pretty little arch of gray stone, wide enough for a carriage, and yet now the moat was more like a river, deep and wild and roiling with foam, with no real way across.

"The bridge is gone," she said, confused.

"That's a really wide moat." Tiana closed one eye and cocked her head as if gauging their chances of getting across. "Too deep to wade, too fast to swim."

"But there has to be a bridge." Snow White paced back and forth, hand in a fist around her pickaxe. "We came all this way, we fought our way here to the castle beyond the mountains, and now there's no way across?"

"There's always a way," Tiana reminded her. "Just not generally the easy one you expected."

Rapunzel sighed sadly. "Even my hair's not long enough to get us across, and I can't make it grow any faster. We'll just have to keep walking around the moat until we find a bridge or a big tree or a nice bar full of rowdy people who look scary but are actually quite kind and have a boat."

Shoulders slumped. Smiles turned to frowns. The pep was absent from steps. All their excitement at reaching their goal drained out as they realized there was no visible way to get past the heaving, frothing moat.

"Left or right?" Tiana asked Snow White.

"Oh! You're . . . asking me?"

"Well, you know this place best. It seems to respond to you, so that makes you the one to ask."

Snow White knelt and put a hand to the ground, but this particular patch of earth didn't know how to help her. It felt like rubbing the belly of a sleeping cat—pleasant but pretty useless.

"I don't know the right way to go, but I know that the river that feeds the moat is usually on the left, so I think right is the better choice," she finally said.

"Right it is. Now pass out those apples and let's go find the mirror." Tiana held her hand out, and Snow White shined an apple on her sleeve and passed it over with a smile. Even if things were miserable, being with her new friends made it bearable.

It was so frustrating, being so close to the castle . . . and so utterly unable to reach it. Snow White knew it was entirely possible that the Queen or her minions might be watching them from any one of dozens of windows. She knew that any moment, a score of hunters or goons, or both, might descend upon them. And yet, what choice did they have? All they could do was circle the castle until they found a way in.

For hours they walked, the castle always in sight, nearly in throwing distance for Sulley, even, and yet there was no sign of a bridge. Finally the hilly forest led them downward, to where the land flattened out near the moat.

"Wait, I know this place!" Snow White said, hurrying forward.

The forest opened up to a small clearing, and there, in the middle of a carpet of green grass surrounded by blossoming cherry trees, was a familiar wishing well. When she'd last sung into the clear, cold water, surrounded by adoring doves and dreaming of a better life, the well had been attached to the castle proper, part of the courtyard near the steps that led up to the throne room. But now, it was as if the castle had pulled itself away from the forest and all things wild and green and true, tucking itself into the moat and leaving the well behind to fend for itself.

"It's not quite where it's supposed to be, but this is where I met the Prince," she said, blushing. "I was singing, and then he joined me. . . ." She sighed. "Things were simpler then. The Queen made every day as terrible as she could, and yet there were little moments of mercy where I could hope and dream."

"You can still hope and dream," Tiana reminded her. "Because we're going to save this place, and you're going to march right on back to the Prince and grab your future by the horns."

"Oh I wouldn't want to grab anything by the horns!" Snow White said.

"Good," Sulley grumbled. "Because it doesn't feel nice."

Tiana flicked her fingers. "Y'all know what I mean. You got to take charge, girl. You're the one who controls your destiny. Not the Queen, not the Fractured Mirror. You."

Snow White laughed and looked away. "I suppose we'll have to see how I feel after I face her, then." She looked down at her pickaxe. "I certainly never saw myself coming after her in her own castle, holding a weapon, so perhaps things really are changing."

"Say, how's this thing work?" Rapunzel asked, leaning over the well. "Hello?"

"Hello?" the well called back in a voice very much like her own.

"Oh, it's a wishing well," Snow White explained. "If you sing to it and it sings back, that means your wish will come true. I wished to meet the one I would love, and the Prince appeared as if out of nowhere." She sighed blissfully. "It really is magical."

Rapunzel's eyes sparkled with excitement. "Mind if I try it?"

"Oh, yeah, no, go ahead," Hades said, rolling his eyes. "When I'm on a mission to save the world from swiftly encroaching evil, I often stop to sing at water. It's just good horse sense."

But Rapunzel ignored him, her curiosity stronger than his ridicule. She leaned over, sticking the entire top half of her body into the well. As if she'd sprung some sort of trap, the branches of the flowering trees shot into the ground, weaving together to form a thickly woven fence of decaying blossoms around the wishing well. The Guardians stumbled back so they wouldn't be impaled by the rushing roots and sharply pointed branches. More branches shot upward, twining together to create an impenetrable dome. Snow White ran up and tried to pry the branches apart, but it only made the snakelike wood pull together more tightly.

They'd been entirely separated from the wishing well—and one of their own.

"Rapunzel?" Snow White called.

But there was no answer.

———◇———

19

Rapunzel loved magical things. And magical places. And wishes, which were always magical. After a long night on the hard ground and a challenging morning fighting a Fractured goddess with great hair on the side of a mountain, she was delighted to encounter something as fascinating and promising as a wishing well. The water glimmered down below, the stones at her feet cool and bedecked with pretty green moss that tickled between her bare toes.

Snow White had said to sing about what she wished for and see if the well sang back, so she cleared her throat and sang.

"I wish to find the Fractured Mirror and save Snow White's home!"

Her words echoed down prettily, and then, much to her initial delight, the sound came back.

"You can't, you fool; you're all alone," her voice replied with a mocking tone.

That . . . was not at all how it should've worked.

She stood back up, the stones still ringing with the word *alone*.

Alone, alone, alone.

"I think it's broken, Snow," she said.

But Snow White was gone.

And the Guardians along with her.

The well was now surrounded by a densely woven carpet of dying blossoms clinging to thick thorny branches. Overhead, yet more branches met, interlaced like a basket and shot through with crisp purple cracks. Sunlight dappled down around her. She was trapped.

"Snow White? Tiana? Everyone? Where are you?" she called.

The only answer was mocking laughter from the well.

She looked down at the water, which moved as if fish flicked their tails just under the surface. Less certain this time, she sang, "I wish my friends would all come back?"

"They won't, because of all you lack," the well replied.

Rapunzel slammed her fists against the stone. "Stop it! Those are lies!"

After a snicker, the well sang, "You're silly and unwise."

She picked up a stone and looked down in the water, where her own reflection glared back at her, furious. With all her might, she hurled the stone down, and it slapped into the water, breaking up her image and sending little ripples to lap against the sides of the wall. But as she watched, the water kept swirling and shifting, as if some fish much larger than it had any right to be was angry and thrashing just beneath the surface. The glimmering liquid began to glow with a familiar purple light.

Before Rapunzel could draw back from this horror, a purple tentacle shot up out of the water, wrapping around her wrist and yanking her down. She fought back, pulling with all her might, but another tentacle appeared and curled around her other wrist, and together, they pulled her inexorably toward the stone rim. Yanking and twisting, tugging and howling, Rapunzel was pulled inch by inch toward the well.

"Hurry, Pascal! Jump out!" she shouted, and the chameleon struggled out of her pocket and leapt out onto the stone right as she tumbled over the lip, head-first into the well.

It was a short fall, and as she plunged underwater, her only thought was to get right side up again. Her wrists were still captured, but she tucked into a ball and held her breath as she used the wall of the well to walk herself around in a somersault, the stone freezing cold against her bare feet. For a terrifying moment, she was trapped entirely under the water, her eyes squeezed shut, and the memory of the cave-in with Eugene threatened to overwhelm her again—that horrifying sensation of being trapped in the darkness, surrounded by unforgiving rock and thundering water with the air swiftly running out. But then she remembered getting through the more recent cave-in with the Guardians, remembered that she had to keep going, and she steeled her heart, finished the flip, and managed to get her head above the surface. She sucked in a huge breath and opened her eyes.

Slowly, like an alligator rising to the surface, a glowing purple shape emerged to face her. It was familiar, yet so wrong.

It was Rapunzel herself . . . but Fractured.

Rapunzel tried to hold up her hands to defend herself, but the hair of her Fractured doppelgänger yanked her arms down tight to her sides.

"No one cared that you went missing," the Fractured said in a voice so very different from her own. Its eyes were a glowing, empty white, its hair matted down around its face.

"Yes they did! My parents cared! They looked for me for years and never forgot the lantern ceremony on my birthday!"

As she shouted, she thrashed, trying to pull her wrists away and kicking with her feet. But the Fractured Rapunzel simply sent out more tendrils of glowing purple hair, capturing her ankles and wrapping her legs just as tightly as her arms. The stone walls of the well were likewise shot with treacherous violet cracks and seemed somehow to narrow with every passing moment, as if the column of stone hoped to swallow her down into the darkness like a giant snake.

"No one cared," the Fractured Rapunzel whispered again, this time slowly and with emphasis.

"They did! They do! I have Pascal and Eugene and Maximus. And the Guardians and Snow White. Mickey chose me!"

The Fractured goon looked up, its cold, still face gazing all about the well as if to illustrate that no one was there. "No. One. Cared."

Tears pricked Rapunzel's eyes as she twisted and growled and grunted, trying to escape the cold, impersonal clutches of her own hair turned evil. It was impossible to fight, impossible to pull away. The goon's purple-lipped mouth turned up at the corners, and then she felt it—the tendrils of hair around her ankles, pulling her down, down, under the water and deeper down into the well. She kicked with all her might and dug her bare toes into the tightly wrapped hair, but it didn't budge. Her chin went under, and then she tipped her head back, gasping for breath as the water slopped up over her ears and toward her nose. With one last, mighty breath, she disappeared under the surface.

Her eyes popped open as she looked for some way, any way, to get free. She didn't know how long she could hold her breath, but she knew it wasn't long. Memories of the cave-in threatened to overwhelm her with every passing second; it was even worse without Eugene here, and she longed to see him one last time. The sides of the well were gray with speckled green moss that waved gently among the glowing purple cracks as she churned the water with her attempts to escape. When she looked up, she saw glimpses of sunlight shining through. And . . . a flash of bright yellow?

There, clinging to the stones, just above the water, was Pascal.

And he wasn't his usual green—he was a bright, glowing gold.

He saw her watching him, and he used his little mitten hand to point at his head.

Rapunzel shook her own head. What was the chameleon trying to tell her?

Now he pointed at his chest, then at his head, then down at her head.

Gold. Hair. Head.

That was it! She had to use her own hair! Why hadn't she thought of that on her own?

Probably because she was about to drown.

She opened her mouth to thank him, but water rushed in, and she sputtered and felt her lungs burn. She didn't have much time left.

She refocused on the Fractured goon, which stared at her with its dead eyes. Snorting the water out of her nose, she reached out with her own prehensile hair, using it to pry away the Fractured purple hair around her wrists and arms and ankles. Her golden hair glowed as it swirled around the well, probing here and there like plant roots seeking a hold between hard stones. The Fractured goon's face faltered, its smug grin disappearing as first one of Rapunzel's ankles and then the other was released from its tentacled grasp. Rapunzel kicked up to the surface and inhaled a big gulp of air, her feet kicking relentlessly so the doppelgänger couldn't catch her again.

With a precision she hadn't needed before, coils of her hair slunk around the Fractured hair, like two octopuses fighting, tugging and prying until her arms were free, then at last her wrists. She was treading water now, holding her head up and taking deep breaths in case she got yanked down again. With a mighty kick, she landed a shot in the Fractured goon's belly, distracting it as her hair shot up toward the stone columns at the top of the well, where it wrapped around them like vines and rooted among the stones. She reached up, grasping the familiar golden hair and climbing up, hand over hand, digging her feet into the wet coils until she was out of the water. The Fractured goon reached for her, and she grinned as she kicked it in the face.

"No one cares about *you*!" she shouted.

She jerked her chin at Pascal, and he dove back into

her pocket. "Thanks, buddy," she murmured, and she heard the flap of his tiny tongue.

As she climbed up one long rope of her hair, the rest of it turned the tide on the Fractured goon, wrapping its arms and legs and holding it tightly as she dragged herself up over the lip of the well. Once her feet were on the ground, she unhooked her frying pan and squared off with the well, her feet making mud of the dust.

Inch by inch, her hair dragged the Fractured Rapunzel out of the well. It kicked and pulled and clung to the stones like a bug, but she tangled her hair with its hair and dislodged it from every crack it tried to cling to. Finally the Fractured was delivered up and out of the well, Rapunzel's hair depositing it on the stones at her feet.

"This doesn't seem fair, but neither did pulling me into the well," she said, rearing back with her frying pan. With each hit, the goon crackled with energy and tried to fight back, but it was so tightly trussed with her hair that it could neither escape nor deal any blows against her. Thanks to her anger and lack of any real opposition, it soon exploded into a pile of crackling purple crystals. The moment before that final hit would probably haunt her forever. It was impossible to forget she was fighting a version of herself, and even if it was evil and unfeeling and senseless, it was still her own face staring up at her.

Her hair, which had been holding down the goon, collapsed in a soggy, relieved heap, and Rapunzel hooked her pan back on her belt.

"Okay, so I don't like wells anymore," she said to herself. "Aaaand I already didn't like caves." She reached into her pocket and withdrew Pascal, kissing him on his head and making him turn pink. "It's a good thing we play charades a lot. You saved me down there, buddy. I owe you a dozen strawberries."

Pascal coolly held out both of his little mitten hands and flashed his fingers.

"Okay, a hundred strawberries." She looked around the flowered dome that contained them. "But first we've got to get out of here."

As if on cue, a glowing shape exploded through the dome, and Stitch, wreathed in flames, hit the stones hard and bounced a few times before skidding to a stop against the wall of branches. Where he'd come through, a scorched hole remained, the edges smoking slightly. Sulley's head appeared.

"You good, Punzy?"

"Aside from being called 'Punzy,' yeah." She leaned down, squeezing water out of the lengths of her hair. "I just got pulled down into the well by my own evil twin, who tried to drown me. With her hair! I can't believe there's a Fractured version of me. I didn't know that could happen! I always knew I was my own worst enemy, but wow! This gal takes the cake. You all doing okay?"

Stitch stood and shook himself, sending slobber flying. "Bad flowers," he said.

"Tell me about it." Rapunzel walked over to the Stitch-sized hole he'd left in the woven branches. "Hades, can you, I don't know, burn this hole bigger?"

Hades walked over, blue flames appearing in both of his hands. "I dunno, maybe." As he touched branches, setting them aflame, he said, "So tell me about this evil twin. How evil was she?" The branches were taking their time burning, so he closed his hands into fists, extinguishing his flames. "Look, let's just do this the easy way."

His arm turned to gray smoke and elongated, reaching through the hole to grab Rapunzel around the waist. She recoiled slightly at the touch of the prehensile limb, but he easily manipulated her through the hole in the branches and set her lightly on the ground.

The smoke retracted back into an arm, which he shook, sending water flying.

"You're very moist. Horrible word, but it fits. Ugh."

Stitch jumped through the hole on his own, turning a neat somersault before landing beside Rapunzel. She sighed in annoyance and braided her sopping hair as well as she could, then looped it over her shoulders.

"For the record, I don't recommend fighting Fractured versions of yourself. They fight dirty." She looked around the forest. "Did you all find a bridge?"

"No, but I think I can make one." Sulley pointed to where an old tree leaned over the moat. "Do you think it'll mind, Snow? I never really thought about whether or not trees had feeling before, but you seem like you would know."

Snow White didn't have to touch the tree to know that there wasn't much hope for it. "It's mostly dead already," she said with a little shrug. "The forest understands we all have to make sacrifices. And I'm sure it'll make a lovely burrow for some appreciative tortoise or badger."

Sulley spit on his paws, shook his whole body, jumped up and down, and then bounded toward the tree and slammed into it with his armored shoulder. There was a loud crack, and the tree obligingly fell, just

tall enough to span the moat. There was indeed a huge hole where its root ball stood up that looked ready-made for an animal to move right on in.

"Is everyone ready?" Tiana asked.

And when everyone nodded, they headed for the new bridge that would take them over the rushing water and up to the evil queen's castle.

———◇———

20

Once they were over the bridge, they stopped for a moment to distribute healing potions, cheese, and some grapes Snow White had found growing among the castle's stonework.

"It used to be ever so much tidier than this," she said. "Beautiful white stone, towers, gardens. Perhaps it will return to itself once the Fractured Magic is gone." She missed this place, where she'd begun life with a doting father and a loving mother, the first queen. She'd looked upon the family portraits and seen a noble woman who'd wanted the best for her people and her daughter. She'd seen a generous and kind king who'd

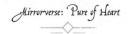

given his little princess everything she'd ever desired.

And then, all too soon, the new queen moved in and those portraits disappeared to some dusty attic, or perhaps the dungeon. And then the king died, and the Queen burned those portraits, along with Snow White's collection of toys and beautiful dresses and pretty tiaras. She'd given the distraught, grieving little girl rags and clogs to wear, handed her a mop and a bucket. And even then, Snow White hadn't hated her—she'd never hated anyone. But she'd felt so alone, so unloved, so hopeless.

And now she was returning to the castle that had been taken from her so long ago, and she was surrounded by friends and filled with a newfound power of her own. The pickaxe in her hands felt like an extension of her body, a gift of the forest, a promise of redemption. As she led the Guardians up the stairs to the castle's kitchen, she hoped she herself was good enough, and that she could possibly live up to the trust Mickey had placed in her, but she knew that the Guardians would have her back no matter what, and that their combined might had gotten them this far.

She motioned for her friends to be quiet at she tiptoed through the empty kitchens, the floors unswept and the ovens cold without her there to do the work. As dramatically as the forest had changed, the interior of the castle seemed to be the same, and she stopped right outside the door that led to the Queen's throne room, alert for any sign of life—or Fractured goons.

"Do you think Snow White is safe?" someone asked from within, and her heart swelled with relief and fondness as she recognized the familiar voice of Happy.

"Oh, well, now, I certainly hope so," Doc said. "But you don't have to keep asking me. I don't have any more information than you do, or than I did mive finutes ago—I mean, five ago minutes—I mean, you know what I mean. . . ."

"Dopey's worried," Happy went on.

"We all are," Doc assured him.

The sound accompanying their voices had to be the clink of chains, and Snow White knew she should've hung back, should've been smart and cunning and quiet, but she had to help her friends. She darted out into the throne room and directly toward where all seven of them were chained to the wall of what had once been the grand hearth of the royal banquet hall. Now it was cold and dark, the fire long gone out; the sun shone weakly through the dust-dimmed colors of the once-beautiful stained glass.

"I'm here!" she called to them. "Oh, you poor things!"

She hurried to Happy's side to get a better look at the chains, but they required a key she did not possess.

"Snow White! You're all right!" Happy said, grinning, living up to his namesake.

"Oh, but you should go!" Doc warned her. "The Queen—"

"Has been here all along," a cruel, arrogant voice intoned.

Snow White spun around to find her wicked stepmother, the Queen, gliding out of a shadowy corner on the dais, her robes blending into the darkness. She was as regal as ever, her smile just as cruel, but her sedate robes had been replaced by a more battle-worthy costume: a high-collared, armored cloak over slim leggings and tall boots. There were strange shadows on her face that reminded Snow White of cruel vines curling up from her throat.

Beside her stood an enormous mirror that seemed to suck all the light and beauty in the room into its crackling vortex. It was as big as the Stellar Mirror in Mirrorforge Crater, big enough to step into, and dominated the space with a frenzied, pulsing energy. Its black frame was riddled with violet cracks, and it hummed with rage and hatred. If the Stellar Mirror's swirls of pink and blue promised new journeys to glorious lands, the Fractured Mirror promised untold horrors and an endless line of enemies, spit out like snake venom.

Snow White was surprised her stepmother would consent to having something so commanding in her own throne room; the Queen liked to be the center of attention, after all, and the mirror certainly stole the show.

"Ahem." The Queen's red lips curled up in a smug, knowing smile. "Surprised to see me?" she asked.

Snow White's instinct was to apologize, to grovel, to back away. But that was no longer the role she had to play in this throne room. She was not some child to be bossed around, unable to fight back against every cruel word that came her way.

"Considering you stole my kingdom and my inheritance and cling to this castle like a spider, I can't say I'm surprised to see you, no," Snow White said, her voice barely trembling. "I came here to find you and put a stop to this—this madness!"

The Queen's eyebrows rose. "Oh, I know, child. I meant for you to come here all along. I've lured you here every step of the way. Now, where are your little friends?"

The Guardians emerged from the kitchen, weapons at the ready, looking determined.

"We're right here, and we're ready to fight you," Tiana said. "That mirror doesn't belong to you, and we're going to destroy it."

The Queen chuckled, the sinister sound echoing throughout the hall. She clapped her hands, and every door to the throne room slammed shut, the bolts snapping down, trapping them. "And what are you going to do, take it away from me? Escape me? Do you have any idea of the power contained in its broken face?"

"I know what it can do." Tiana took a potion out of her bag and tossed it up in the air, catching it neatly. "The question is: do you know what *we* can do? Because we're not scared of your little goons. We've been destroying them all along."

"As per my plan." The Queen strode to the mirror and caressed it with a gloved hand. The shiny surface took on a dead white glow, and an army of Fractured goons filed out, each leaping to the floor and moving aside until a dozen goons were arranged around the Queen, their gleaming white eyes empty and their weapons ready. "Each obstacle you faced was designed to uniquely challenge each of you so that I could discover whose heart is truly the purest one of all."

Rapunzel stepped forward, frying pan in hand. "Why do you care about pure hearts when yours is obviously not?"

The Queen slunk toward them, and they all readied their weapons, bouncing on their feet as they prepared for some sort of attack. Much to Snow White's surprise, the Queen reached for her black glove, tugging on each finger as she spoke. "Because a pure heart is the only way to counteract the poison flowing through this land—and through me." She pulled off her glove, revealing her once smooth white hand, now riddled with acid green veins that writhed like earthworms in a rainstorm.

"Oh my!" Snow White said, shocked. "Did the Fractured Magic do that?"

The Queen glared at her. "No. When the first wave of magic crashed over our world, I was creating a very potent poison for . . ." She raised one perfect eyebrow at Snow White. "Let's say, someone in particular. But as you know, that magic changed things, amplified them. The shock of that wave made the earth quake, and my cauldron spilled its bubbling brew. Some landed on my hand, some landed on the ground. And then its insidious work began as it burrowed deeper into my body—and into this world." Her hand strayed up to the shadowy streaks reaching up from the throat of her cloak as if trying to devour her whole.

"And you think a human heart can fix it?" Tiana asked, arms crossed.

The Queen nodded. "Not necessarily human, but yes. I have consulted my grimoire. One among you possesses the magic that can heal this poison. You can feel it inside you, like a glowing warmth. Step forward and sacrifice yourself so that the others might live, and this world can be renewed. Banish my poison, and I will banish the Fractured Mirror." With her hideous hand, she reached to her belt and withdrew a jeweled dagger.

Snow White hurried to join the Guardians as they circled up to confer in hurried whispers. "Do you think she's telling the truth?" she asked her friends. "I'll admit, she's not known for her honesty."

"We can't deny that the green poison we've seen out there matches her hand—" Tiana began.

"Ick, right?" Hades said with a shiver of distaste. "I see dead people, and they're a lot less disgusting than that lizard hand."

Pascal blew a tiny, insulted raspberry from Rapunzel's shoulder.

"I said she's grosser than you," Hades told him. "So, you're winning."

"You know"—Sulley scratched his head, dislodging several leaves—"she said her poison is infecting the land, but it's really only infected people and animals she's sent to hurt us."

"That's true," Snow White allowed. "But the way the shape of things has changed—like the jagged canyons and the raging moat—those things weren't Fractured. Maybe her poison is inside of things, warping them."

"Ticktock," the Queen called. "If you won't step up for the land, step up for this sniveling fool."

Snow White heard a gasp and a whimper and looked up. The Queen's dagger was under Dopey's chin, its point pressing into his throat.

"It doesn't matter if it's true or not," Snow White said softly. "She'll kill him. She'll kill all of them, if she can. She says she needs a heart, but she herself is heartless."

"Someone step forward, or he's the first to go," the Queen warned.

Dopey began crying, and Grumpy shouted, "You won't get away with this, you lily-livered bully!"

Snow White's heart was pounding, her chest tight with rage. She longed to fight the Queen, hand to hand, but knew that by the time she crossed the room, Dopey would've already paid the price. "We have to do something!"

"If someone has to sacrifice themself, it should be me," Tiana said firmly. "Mickey told me my job was to support you all, to keep you going even when you thought you couldn't go on. I'm a healer. And if this land—and this terrible woman—need healing, then I should be the one to do it."

"No way!" Rapunzel stepped forward, grabbing Tiana by the shoulders. "You're practically our leader. Whenever we don't know what to do next, we look to you. The group needs you. But I'm just some girl with a frying pan and a lot of hair. I'm expendable. Although Pascal is not."

Tiana shook her head. "Just because that's what Gothel told you every day of your life doesn't make it true. You're like . . . the frosting that holds a cake together. We need you."

"Then maybe it's me," Sulley said, setting down his shield. "I'm doing everything I can to save my own world, but I'm not enough. This place needs a hero. All those animals, that big forest—they need a champion.

And let's be honest—when it comes to size, my heart's probably the size of a watermelon, and yours is more like a plum. Mine has more, uh . . ."

"Blood?" Hades offered.

"More return on investment," Sulley finished with a shrug.

"No, Stitch," Stitch said, shouldering his way to the center of the circle. "I . . . change mass. Heart can change. Lilo said—uh—unusual amount of badness. Queen likes badness. Yes?" He pantomimed something with his top hands that didn't quite make sense, as if measuring something from the ground up.

"You're all so kind and generous and brave," Snow White said with tears in her eyes. "This isn't even your world, and yet you'd die for it. I used to sing to the wishing well that I wanted a hero, and now I have all of you." She touched Stitch's cheek, Sulley's softly furred shoulder, Rapunzel's arm, Tiana's hand, looking into each of their eyes as if trying to burn them into her memory forever. Hades stayed a bit back, nostrils flared in disgust at the excess of feeling, so she just smiled at him and hoped he would understand.

"But this is my world, and it's my responsibility," she went on. "Everything that's happened here was to lure me closer so the Queen could finally claim my heart. I'm what she wants, what she's always wanted. I'm what this place requires. And let's face it. You're all Guardians. You're special. Other worlds need you. Mickey needs you. I'm just . . ." She looked down at her fine boots, her leaf skirt, her pickaxe, but she was recalling a torn, stained skirt and dirty clogs. "I'm just a scullery maid."

"Why, that's ridiculous!" Doc shouted from across the room.

"Yes, you're so much more than that!" Happy chimed in.

"What a buncha no-good claptrap!" Grumpy added.

Tiana stepped forward and held Snow White by the upper arms. "They're right. You were never just a scullery maid. You were always special. Even when people told you you weren't, when they tried to put you down and make you believe you deserved mistreatment. You have always been a bright, brave soul and a good friend."

Happy, Doc, Bashful, Sleepy, Sneezy, and Grumpy, all cheered their agreement, and the Guardians nodded and wiped away rogue tears.

"That might be the nicest thing anyone's ever said to me," Snow White said sadly, shaking her head and wiping her eyes. "And it makes me all the more determined that this is my destiny."

She turned to face the Queen, setting down her pickaxe and raising her chin.

"I guess you get what you always wanted," she said to her stepmother. "My heart in your hand, your beauty reigning supreme."

The Queen's grin was a wide and vicious thing.

"Finally, child, you talk sense. Come to me and let us finish this."

But she didn't take the knife away from Dopey's throat; if anything, she pressed it in deeper to urge Snow White forward.

Each step across the great hall felt like it took an hour, Snow White's boots clicking on the stone that she'd so often scrubbed clean on her hands and knees well into the night. She comforted herself with thoughts of her seven friends, back home in their snug cottage, comfortable and safe. She imagined the forest returning to its glossy green best, to the animals playing in the sunshine, fat and fed, the fawns frolicking without a care in the world. This, she thought, was a good way to go, if one had to go.

But then something poked her in the chest, stopping her in her tracks and making her stumble backward. It looked like smoke, but it felt like a hand.

"Wait a minute," Hades boomed. "What about me?"

"What about you?" the evil queen coldly replied. "You have no dominion here."

"Well, everybody else did their little self-sacrifice speech and got all teary and boo-hoo, but what about me? You want purity of heart? Oh, baby, have I got purity of heart."

Snow White turned around in absolute shock to watch as Hades reached into his misty robes and pulled out . . . a beating heart wreathed in blue flames. "Here. See for yourself."

Without another word, he threw his heart at the Queen.

———◇———

21

Hades's heart, writhing with blue flame, exploded against the Queen's chest, knocking her into the wall and sending her knife skittering across the stone floor. Unharmed, Dopey fell to sitting, his chains rattling as he softly cried. As if on cue, the Fractured goons attacked.

"Don't you need your heart?" Rapunzel asked as she focused on a charging goon and spun her frying pan.

Hades shrugged as he prepared a palm-sized ball of flames. "Fire is a pretty renewable resource for me. I've got plenty. Plus, you know—I'm the god of the

Underworld. What am I going to do—die?" He lobbed his flaming projectile at one goon and grabbed another with his elongated smoke arm, preparing to beat it into shards as if he hadn't just done something completely impossible.

Even if he was a god, even if it was flame . . . didn't he need his heart?

Apparently not. He didn't slow down, didn't falter as he threw himself into battle with a new determination. Each of the Guardians waded into the melee, raining down hit after hit on the goons, but Snow White had other plans. Hefting her pickaxe, she landed a solid swing on the goon facing her, and while it stumbled back, sparking with electricity, she darted around it and ran toward the old hearth.

With the Queen slumped on the floor, her seven friends were unguarded. She ran directly to Doc.

"Is there a key?" she asked, inspecting the manacle that chained him to the wall.

"Why, I don't know," Doc said. "Look out!"

Snow White spun around to find that the goon had followed her, determined to finish the fight.

"Oh, honestly! Can't you see I'm busy?"

She squared off with the goon, swinging her pickaxe

around in elegant arcs and jabs until her foe exploded. Once it was no more than a pile of shards, she turned back to her friends.

"I'm going to use my pickaxe," she said. "You'll probably want to look away."

Each of her friends was chained to the wall with a single chain and manacle. She gently took Doc's hand and placed the manacle against the stone wall.

"Are you sure that's going to work?" Doc asked worriedly. "That's an awfully pig bickaxe. I mean, big pickaxe."

"She's had a lot of experience using it," Tiana shouted as she threw potions at the nearest enemy. "Your girl fought her way here through a dozen goons, mutated squirrels, an ensorcelled huntsman, attacking princes, endless chasms, raging godlings, you name it."

"Oh, my!" Doc said, his eyes shining. "Why, I always knew you had it in you!"

He held his hand still and turned away, and Snow White worried that she might strike the metal wrong or hurt Doc . . . but Tiana was right. She knew her weapon, knew how to aim. There was no reason to worry or doubt herself. She could do this.

Rearing back, she struck the manacle with the tip

of her pickaxe, and the metal fell to the ground in two pieces, trailing its chain. Doc stared at his hand, turning it this way and that as he blinked in shock.

"Well, Jiminy Cricket!" he said. "Stat's thupendous! I mean, uh, that is, that's stupendous! Who's next, boys?"

Dopey held out the hand that wasn't manacled, nodding his head so hard that his hat slipped down over his tear-stained eyes.

"Of course, Dopey," Snow White said fondly, taking the manacled hand and placing it against the wall instead. "Now, don't move!"

With a perfectly aimed swing, she struck the manacle off, freeing Dopey, who began dancing around and tripped over Grumpy's feet.

"Reckon I'll go next," he grumbled. "Dungeons make my calluses ache."

After Grumpy came Sneezy, who pulled his hand away to sneeze, making Snow White lodge her pickaxe in the wall. Then Happy, who didn't cause a single problem at all and was just, well, happy to no longer be shackled to the Queen's hearth. Then Sleepy, who was possibly the easiest to help of all, as he slept through the whole thing. Last came Bashful, who kept looking away and blushing—but at least he held his hand still. Finally all of them were free and Snow White was able to turn her attention back to the fight.

"To the kitchen, everyone!" Doc called, and he led the charge around the goons and into the kitchen. Snow White was relieved to think they were wisely staying out of the battle . . . until they returned, howling fiercely, holding cleavers and bread knives and meat tenderizers, ready to do their part to vanquish the enemies.

The battle raged as the Guardians turned fighting into an art, each of them using their weapons and abilities to skillfully carve their way around the throne room. The sound of shattering goons punctuated the air at regular intervals, and when Snow White ran to the next goon, purple shards crunched under her boots. She slashed it across the chest with her pickaxe, but it managed to catch her on the leg, making her stumble backward. She desperately needed to focus, and yet her attention was torn in multiple directions.

On one hand, she couldn't stop watching Doc and the boys gang up on a goon. It was absolutely imperative that none of her friends got hurt, but they were brave and strong and true, and she had to respect their desire to help foil the villains. Ever since she'd shown up at their cottage, they'd felt responsible for her, had pledged to help her and keep her safe . . . and yet now she felt responsible for them. With her newfound abilities, she needed to protect her friends, no matter the cost.

On the other hand, she kept looking back over her shoulder to where the Queen lay splayed on the ground. This woman had torn her life apart, sent her out into the woods to die, and deliberately set traps to test and possibly kill her. And yet Snow White couldn't help feeling sorry for her and worrying that she would take damage in the fray. It was an odd way to feel, but that was apparently who Snow White was: someone who cared deeply for others, even when they perhaps did not deserve it.

"We fanquished the voe! Er, I mean, we veat the billain! Fought the villain! We won!" Doc shouted, and everyone raised a kitchen implement and cheered, except Dopey, who just stuck his wooden spoon in his mouth to lick off something that looked suspiciously like honey.

Comforted to know they were competent against the goons, Snow White looked to the next one . . . but the last two goons were already surrounded on all sides by the Guardians, buzzing with energy as they took hit after hit. Happy, Sleepy, Dopey, Doc, Bashful, Sneezy, and Grumpy hurried to do their part, and the goons didn't have a chance—not that they'd ever had a chance under such an onslaught. As Snow White rushed to join her friends and end the threat, she noticed something odd.

Hades wasn't fighting. He was standing off to the side, alone, stroking his chin contemplatively. And yes, sure, the fight was almost done and he wasn't desperately needed, but it still wasn't the kind of behavior she expected out of a prospective Guardian. Maybe losing his heart really had hurt him.

"Hades, aren't you going to help?" she asked. "Are you hurt?"

He looked to her and winked, then ran across the room . . . right toward the dais. Leaping up the stone stairs, he stepped up to the Fractured Mirror and stroked a smoky finger lovingly down its frame.

"I feel like I've done my civic duty," he said, voice ringing to fill the throne room. "And maybe I finally found my purpose. Look, you guys are okay. Not great, but okay. We had some fun times. But I think this mirror is going to be a lot more fun. I can make my own

friends. And they'll never argue with me." His grin curled up, his eyes alight with mischief. "Because goons only say exactly what they're told to say. Bye!"

At his command, a swirl of elemental energy appeared and coalesced into a portal, which swallowed up Hades and the Fractured Mirror like a whirlpool. In a crack of thunder, they both disappeared.

Hades and the Fractured Mirror . . . were gone.

———◇———

22

"What was that?" Tiana asked, looking up as the final goon exploded in a shower of purple crystals. She glanced around the room and did a double take when she got to the dais. "What, where's the mirror?"

"Hades took it," Snow White said, head hanging as if this were somehow her fault.

"I guess he wasn't Guardian material after all." Tiana shook her head. "Mickey's going to be so disappointed. He really thought there was a chance we could turn Hades around."

"Bad guys gonna bad guy," Rapunzel said, dusting purple shards out of her hair. "At least he didn't actively hurt us. Just took advantage of us to steal the mirror that brings havoc and decay to every world in which it appears." She sighed. "No, when I say it like that, it definitely sounds like he actively hurt us."

"I didn't trust that guy at first, but he was really winning me over!" Sulley stomped a foot. "And now he's a villain again? I thought blue guys were supposed to stick together!"

Stitch tugged on his own blue fur, and said, "Stitch stick." Sulley gently fist-bumped him.

"Well, even if we didn't take control of the mirror and return it to Mickey, at least it can't make any more goons right now," Tiana said, looking around the ruins of the throne room, the tables and chairs and pennants destroyed by the fight. "And now that it's gone, this world should go back to normal."

"A pretty sentiment, but it cannot, I'm afraid."

Hearing the Queen's voice, weak as it was, the Guardians ran to stand over her where she lay on her back on the ground, their weapons pointed at her and their faces set in grim determination.

"Yes, go on," she said, her voice thready and weak. "End me. Put me out of my misery that your world may yet again thrive, Fairest of Them All. I thought a pure heart would heal my poisoned blood, but I begin to see that some evils cannot be reversed. This poison is too insidious. Even now, I feel my life ebbing." She held up her hand, and the green veins twisted through it, her knuckles knobbed like those of a crone and her nails brittle talons.

"Well, maybe Hades wasn't the purest of heart," Rapunzel reasoned. "Maybe it really is one of us—"

Tiana snorted. "Why are you giving her ideas? She already got one heart; she can't have two. None of us are giving up our life to *maybe* help a villain who was willing to destroy an entire world for her own selfish purposes. And . . . well, let's just say I'm not feeling too charitable toward villains in general right now. Maybe there are other options, now that she doesn't have her dagger pointed at anyone's throat. Let's try my potion before we make any more hasty decisions."

She dug a now-familiar potion out of her bag and knelt, looking only slightly disgusted as she cradled the Queen's head and unstoppered the tube.

"What is that?" the Queen asked, turning away. "Some cowardly poison, meant to kill me while I am at my weakest?"

"Sorry, sugar, but I'm not the poisoning type." Tiana held the tube against the Queen's stubbornly pinned lips. "This would be the opposite of that. I've used this potion to heal every creature and person you poisoned. ·Even had it used on me in the mine. Now open up and take a sip so I can go home."

At first the Queen resisted, but she was weak as a kitten and couldn't put up much of a struggle.

"Snow, you wanna hold her nose until she opens up?" Tiana asked.

"Such indignity," the Queen complained, and as soon as her mouth was open, Tiana poured the potion down.

The Queen drank, the liquid staining her lips. Everyone waited with bated breath to see what would happen. Even the Queen sat up a little, her eyes unfocused as if she were reaching deep inside herself, waiting for the change to take hold.

But nothing happened.

"You're no witch," she complained, sneering at Tiana. "Your potion has no power."

"Oh, I assure you it does," Tiana shot back. "But trying to heal you with a potion would be like trying to take the salt out of the ocean by tossing in a potato. You're just too full up with poison for a normal dose to have any effect. It might take ten tubes, or it might take a hundred—"

"Maybe she's right," Rapunzel said. "Maybe it really is all about a pure heart. Maybe we need to—"

"No. We're worth more than that. But . . ." Snow White pointed to the object they'd all thus far ignored: Hades's burning blue heart, still lying forgotten on the flagstone, its flames dancing and writhing even with him long gone. "I suppose Hades isn't what you'd call pure, but fire is, and his fire burns on its own. Perhaps there's no permanent antidote, but this heart could still be the key to stopping the poison."

She held a hand out toward Rapunzel. "May I?"

Rapunzel unhooked her frying pan and handed it over, saying, "Just don't use soap. Soap will absolutely destroy the seasoning."

Using her pickaxe, Snow White scraped the fiery heart into the frying pan and held it out to the Queen. "Can you help her sit up, please?" she asked, and Sulley lifted the Queen up as if she were but a doll. It was almost comical, seeing someone so regal and proud forced to sit on the floor like a child, her ostentatious robes splayed around her in the dust and her legs stuck out stubbornly in front of her.

"Try feeding your poison into the heart," she told her wicked stepmother. "Maybe it won't be purged completely, but bit by bit, even your cruelty might fade away. Why, who knows who you might be, without your poison?"

"Even you could be a Guardian one day if you work hard enough," Tiana added.

Snow White grimaced and shook her head. It was a terrible idea. If they couldn't trust Hades, they most certainly couldn't trust the evil queen, who'd already tried to ruin Snow White's life multiple times over the years.

"A Guardian, like you? That sounds insufferable," the Queen said, a trace of her regal bearing returning.

Gingerly she reached her hand into the flames of Hades's heart. She flinched at first, then, realizing it wasn't so bad, turned her hand this way and that in the flames, sighing as if it brought some sort of relief. After a few moments, she held up her hand, and the veins that had once been as green and ropey as ivy vines had faded to a seafoam green almost hidden by the icy white skin.

"That will do," she said, fascinated by the effect and shoving her other hand into the flames.

"Yeah, I'm gonna need my frying pan back," Rapunzel said, fidgeting. "This is not a permanent thing. I'm sure your kitchen will have something similar."

Right on cue, Dopey held up a well-greased pan, ears wiggling in delight, and Snow White transferred

the heart—what a strange thing to say!—into something
to which Rapunzel didn't have an emotional attach-
ment. The Queen didn't seem to care. Not about the
Guardians, not about Snow White. She was mesmerized
by the flames, charmed by her own hands returning to
their former beauty.

"You may go," she said with a jerk of her chin.

Snow White met Tiana's eyes, and Tiana shrugged.
"Sounds like our business is concluded. The fire might
not permanently solve the poison problem, but as long
as it's burning, she can keep feeding the poison into
it and hopefully keep it from infecting the land again.
Unless you want to stick around and nurse her back to
health, I guess we're good to go? Or do you have something you'd like to say to her, Snow?"

That was something Snow White had never considered before—standing up or even talking back to
the Queen. As a little girl, she'd first tried to please
her stepmother, then tried to avoid her, then tried not
to anger her, then had to run from her. But now the
Queen was on the floor, weak and alone, unprotected,
and Snow White realized that while she would absolutely not be sticking around to play nursemaid, she
did, in fact, have something to say.

"When you came to this castle, I thought you were

the most beautiful woman I'd ever seen," she said. "After the portraits of my own mother. And I wanted you to like me. I thought you would take care of me and love me, and that we could play dress-up together, and you would teach me how to be a gracious ruler. But instead you were jealous of me from the start, cruel and belittling and stern. It was as if you found every soft, tender part of me and struck out, trying to hurt me in any way you could. But no matter how terrible you were to me, I never gave up hope that I could have a life where I was liked for who I am. Despite you, I found friends, and I discovered skills and abilities that I never knew I possessed. Not because of you—but despite you. And now I tell you this: I pity you. You could've had love, and instead you chose wickedness. And now you have to live with that, alone, in a castle that could've been filled with laughter and happiness." Snow White looked all around at the dirty stone, the grimy windows, the empty, empty tables. "So enjoy that. Let's go."

But she didn't wait for someone else to lead. She turned her back on the Queen and headed for the nearest door to the garden. Doc, Happy, Sleepy, Bashful, Sneezy, and Grumpy protectively clustered up around her, and Dopey reached out to hold her hand. Stitch took her other hand as the Guardians followed her.

Together, everyone left the Queen's throne room without looking back.

As for the Queen, she didn't even look up.

She had a new obsession, and that was all that had ever mattered.

For Snow White, however, the future . . . was not so clear.

23

As soon as she set foot outside the castle, Snow White could tell that things had changed for the better. Burning the poison out of the Queen must've helped draw it out of the land as well, or perhaps Tiana's potion had had more of an effect than anticipated. The stonework surrounding the castle proper had magically reverted to its original layout, the wishing well exactly where it was supposed to be and no longer surrounded by a living cage of Fractured blossoms and violet-threaded thorns. Doves fluttered down to sing sweetly to Snow White from their perches among the flowering vines as she passed by. The moat was a moat again, sleepy and green and slow, full of frogs and lily pads. The little arched bridge was back, picturesque and sturdy, leading the way to a forest of robust, softly soughing trees free of both purple cracks and dripping green poison.

"Well, this is much nicer," Tiana admitted.

"Oh, yes," Snow White agreed. "The forest is itself again. It's happy. I can sense it, somehow." Two doves flew over and deposited a crown of flowers on her head, and she laughed. "The animals are happy, too. It was horrid, how things were before—just so wrong and twisted."

"That's what happened to us—the bine went merserk!" Doc told her, shaking his head as if to clear it. "The mine, I mean! It went berserk!"

"We was almost to quittin' time," Grumpy continued. "And the darnedest thing happened. These fellers showed up out of nowhere, those same purple animal fellers—and we weren't ready for 'em, so—"

"So they captured us in sacks," Bashful said, looking away. "It were right uncomfortabibble."

"We were so worried about you!" Happy said. "I wasn't feeling happy at all, I can tell you that."

"I was worried about you, too," Snow White told

them. "I came home from the forest, and there were goons who looked just like you in your own beds, but they attacked me!"

"Let me at 'em!" Grumpy jumped around, fists in the air. "Impersonatin' me without my permission!"

"Why, what'd you do?" Sleepy asked with a jaw-cracking yawn.

"Well, I fought them," Snow White said. "I had to! I knew they weren't you, so I had to get rid of them and go find you."

"She fought seven goons by herself and won," Tiana broke in. "Her first fight, too! I must say I'm impressed. And so was Mickey. Just wait until he hears about this adventure."

"Oh, I just did what I had to," Snow White said, unaccustomed to being the center of attention. "I'm just glad my dear friends are free and the mirror's gone. Our world is safe again." She looked to Tiana. "Isn't it?"

"As long as the Queen keeps her poison at bay." Tiana looked grim. "But the thing about the Fractured Mirror is that it jumps from world to world, and wherever it ends up, the Fractured Magic worms its way into the land and the people. So it may be gone from your world, but that just means it's somewhere else, waiting to wreak havoc—and with Hades controlling it."

"Well, what do we do now? Do we go after Hades?"

Tiana looked at her measuringly. "We see what Mickey has to say."

With the Fractured Magic banished and the world set to rights, it was a short and pleasant walk from the castle to the glade where Snow White's journey had begun as she helped splint the broken leg of a fawn. She couldn't help thinking of how far she'd come—and how oddly her world had stretched out, so that the trip to the Queen's castle that should've taken them a few hours had required several days of travel. When they reached the pretty little clearing, the portal they'd arrived in was still there, ready to take them back to Mirrorforge Crater—and Mickey.

"You're coming with us, right?" Rapunzel asked Snow White, who was wringing her hands nervously.

"If you think I should. I don't want to interrupt important business . . ." Snow White began.

"Nonsense!" Tiana said. "You're as much a part of this team as any of us, and Mickey will want to hear the full story. Are you ready?"

Snow White turned back to her friends with a gentle smile. "You go on home to the cottage and make some pancakes," she told them. "I'll be home as soon as I can to help you tidy up."

"We can pidy up tancakes! I mean, tidy up pancakes!" Doc exclaimed. "We're ferfectly punctional. Punctionally ferfect. We can do it ourselves! You go on and visit this Mickey fella."

"I don't like tidying up," Grumpy began. "Agitates my sciatica—"

"Oh, put a sock in it!" Doc said, wagging a finger in Grumpy's face. "Snow White's had a bit of a day! Now let's go. She's got important business."

As Doc led them away, Snow White waved and called, "Goodbye! Get some sleep! And sorry about the broken things! That's a story for later. . . ."

"I like stories!" Happy called. "I can't wait!"

"I don't sleep good unless you're around," Grumpy grumbled.

"Oh, I sleep good no matter what," Sleepy said.

With one last wave, Snow White turned back to the Guardians.

"You first," Stitch said with a little bow.

She stepped toward the swirling portal, and even though she knew what was coming, it was still a surprise to feel it suck her forward and envelop her in billowing sparkles and gentle breezes. With the soft pop of a bubble breaking, she landed lightly in Mirrorforge Crater, quickly stepping out of the way so that whoever came through next would have plenty of room. She did not relish getting accidentally squashed by Sulley.

"Who's this?" someone asked, and Snow White noticed Mickey talking to someone new, a woman dressed warmly in blue edged with white fur, a dramatic cape suggesting she might do well in the Prince's castle. She held a peculiar twisted staff crowned by a glowing red rose, and considering the genesis of her own weapon, Snow White guessed that this new woman had her own tale to tell.

"Belle, meet Snow White," Mickey said with a grin. "Belle is among our first Guardians, and I was just filling her in on your quest. How'd it go? No trouble, I hope, ha ha!"

Tiana leapt nimbly out of the Stellar Mirror and walked over to join the circle. "There's always trouble, or you wouldn't need us. The good news is that Snow White's world is free of Fractured influence. The Queen's poison has been neutralized, although it could be a problem somewhere down the line."

Rapunzel, Sulley, and Stitch came through the mirror, and Mickey stared at it and frowned. "Where's Hades?"

"That's the bad news," Tiana continued. "When he saw the Fractured Mirror and realized what it could do, he stole it. Right after saving all of our lives and possibly the Queen's, too. It happened so fast we couldn't stop him."

Mickey shook his head sadly. "I had such high hopes for him."

"We did, too," Sulley said. "I know I'm blue, but now I feel ultra blue."

"Tiana, can you come chat with Belle and me for a moment?" Mickey said. Snow White just stood there awkwardly until Mickey waved his hands through the air, producing several cozy tuffets and a table covered in treats. "Have a seat and help yourselves! I know you did a great job, and I'm pretty sure you're hungry."

"Always hungry," Stitch and Sulley mumbled at the same time as they stood over the table, drooling.

Tiana patted Snow White on the shoulder and went to join Mickey and Belle. Snow White hurried to load up a small plate before Stitch could slobber on all the cookies.

"Does Mickey always do this after a quest?" she asked.

"Oh, definitely!" Rapunzel said, filling her frying pan with treats. "It's one of the best perks about being a Guardian. Stellar Magic makes the macarons come out juuuuust right."

As they ate, Mickey conferred with Tiana and Belle.

Snow White couldn't stop glancing over, wondering what they were talking about and hoping that she'd done a good enough job. Sure, they'd saved her world, but they'd lost the Fractured Mirror—and Hades. When she'd tasted every flavor of treat on the table, Mickey, Tiana, and Belle came to join the others.

"First of all, I'd like to thank everyone," Mickey began as he stood before the table. "You did a wonderful job. Saving an entire world is no mean feat. I know each of you was uniquely challenged on this assignment, and I commend you for your success. Maybe your hearts aren't pure enough for the Queen, but they're pure enough for me and the Stellar Mirror, ha ha!"

But then his brows drew down. "I know you're as sad as I am that the Fractured Mirror again escaped our grasp. It looks like this fight won't be a short one—or an easy one. That mirror and its dark magic have a way of turning villainous hearts and causing more trouble no matter how skillfully we try to contain it. Despite everyone's hard work, it's clear that the Guardians need more help."

And then he walked to Snow White and held out his hand. She took it and stood, confused.

"Snow White, will you join us and become a Guardian?"

Her jaw dropped, and for a moment all she could do was blink, utterly stunned.

"Me?" she managed.

"I hear you did a splendid job," Mickey said. "Fighting, supporting, helping. You're exactly the kind of person we need to combat the Fractured."

"Oh, I don't know." She looked down. "Do you . . . do you think I'm ready?"

Mickey smiled as he shook his head. "Don't you see? You're so much more than ready. The Stellar Magic recognized the potential in you, augmenting your talents so that you could use your skills and gifts to save your world. That doesn't happen to just anyone. It happens to Guardians."

The Guardians stood to surround her.

"You've got what it takes," Tiana said.

"You never gave up," Sulley added, patting her shoulder with a huge paw.

Rapunzel hip-bumped her. "For someone without a frying pan, you're a darned good fighter!"

"Good stew," Stitch added, although Snow White wasn't sure how that would help her as a Guardian.

"It's unanimous," Mickey proclaimed. "If you'll join us, we'll be glad to have you."

Snow White looked back to the Stellar Mirror and

its mysterious swirls. "But what about my world? My friends at their cottage, the animals, the forest—they need me, and I know now that I need them."

"Think of it like a job," Mickey said. "You'll spend most of your time in your world, but whenever the Fractured Mirror appears, you might be called to join a team that can use your special skills."

"And you can visit other worlds!" Rapunzel said. "You can even go to Tiana's world and eat her beignets!"

Snow White looked from person to person, finding only genuine enthusiasm and happy grins. "I want to thank you all so much for coming to my world and fighting to save it," she began. "It means so much to me that you would leave your own worlds and risk your lives for someone you've never met and a place you've never seen."

"But?" Tiana asked.

Snow White grinned. "But now you'll have to let me return the favor."

A cheer went up, and Stitch bounced around like a rubber ball. Mickey shook Snow White's hand and congratulated her, and everyone spent a little more time with the buffet, which had magically refilled. Tiana passed around healing potions for anyone who'd taken damage in the fight, and Snow White asked to bring some food home for her friends, who had seemingly bottomless stomachs. Even though it seemed as if time didn't exist in Mirrorforge Crater, it suddenly felt as if afternoon was turning to evening. Snow White was the first to yawn, and then it spread from person to person until even Mickey was yawning behind a gloved hand.

"I suppose it's time to go home now," Snow White said.

"It's a temporary goodbye," Rapunzel assured her. "Believe me—there's always some kind of mischief, now that the Fractured Mirror exists."

The group headed toward the Stellar Mirror, hugging goodbye and wishing one another well. Mickey told Snow White he'd give her some time to recover, and then as soon as they knew where Hades had taken the mirror, she might be called on to help track him down. She nodded sleepily and prepared herself for the swirling otherness of the Stellar Mirror.

Epilogue

---◇---

But before Snow White could step forward and feel that sunny tug, the colors began to shift and spin faster and with more urgency. She leapt out of the way right as a huge figure flew out of the mirror and landed, its odd metal wings retracting into a battered, scratched-up suit of white-and-green armor unlike anything Snow White had ever seen. The figure looked all around, then pressed a button that made its helmet glide back to reveal a strong, powerful-looking man with a big chin and worried eyes.

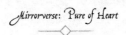

"What's wrong, Buzz?" Mickey asked.

"We've got big trouble," the man said. "This is an intergalactic emergency. The Fractured Mirror—it's back!"

THE END